Unfinished Discussion About God

THE DIARY OF A TIME TRAVELER

mia johansson

Order this book online at www.trafford.com
or email orders@trafford.com

Most Trafford titles are also available at major online book retailers.

Volume translated from Romanian by the MA Program for the Translation
of the Contemporary Literary Text, http://mttlc.ro,

Director: Lidia Vianu. Translators: Elena Bodolan, Cati Godeanu, Mihaela
Grigoras, Alinda Ivanov, Georgiana Mandru, Diana Olteanu, Mona Pinta,
Cora Radu, Cristina Sandu, Manela Stancu, Teodora Tanase.

Original title: "Discutie neterminata despre Dumnezeu – Jurnalul unui Calator in Timp"

Front cover design: Mia Johansson

Front cover and original interior images: Mia Johansson

Printed in the United States of America.

ISBN: 978-1-4907-4843-6 (sc)
ISBN: 978-1-4907-4845-0 (hc)
ISBN: 978-1-4907-4844-3 (e)

Library of Congress Control Number: 2014917959

Trafford rev. 11/12/2014

 www.trafford.com

North America & international
toll-free: 1 888 232 4444 (USA & Canada)
fax: 812 355 4082

To You and Me

Contents

The Jazz and the Blues

It was that year I was born. Was it a newsworthy event? Yes. I was born. Was it historical? Maybe. Cultural? I doubt it, but who knows. Astrological? It must have been since I was born. That means the planets and the stars the whole universe was in harmony giving birth to ME. How was it?Sweat and pain and screaming and yelling. A lot of pain. It must have hurt a lot coming to an unknown place all alone, trying to make my way into the world. And all you see is a light, bright and colored like a rainbow. In fact it is a rainbow. The light. It has all the colors in it. It has everything you want. And something more, Life!

It was quite some time ago but I still remember it. Or maybe… Anyway ever since that day I have started to die a little. Every day we die a little. So strange, isn't it? We are born to start dying. Every second until we finally remember the day we made the step into the unknown. But maybe that day, the final day, we'll remember exactly that moment, The Birth. It is the moment we are (are we?) ready to be reborn and see the light. Again.

There was a lot of talking crap, wasn't there?

"At least you've had a good morning, haven't you?" my neighbor said to me this morning. I suppose he's right, since nothing is personal or private or intimate anymore nowadays.

In fact I did have a good morning today. I managed to get up like every single morning since that very day when I saw the light. And it's a miracle. Just think how marvelous life is; to feel the heart beating, the blood rushing into your veins and the sweat drops trickling-down all over your body. To wake up early in the morning and open your eyes wide into a fabulous new world full of the unexpected. Full of colors, of dance and movement. Of silence
Of Jazz
And Blues

How was I? Naked. Pretty much naked. As I am today. As I was before and shall be tomorrow. I mean, why should we need something so trivial, so useless as some pieces of thread to hide… what?

Us from whom we are, to be sure that we'll succeed and conquer that tiny spot, that short moment we've been given here, that we call life?

That morning I thought it would be as usual; shiny and warm. But it wasn't. The wind started to blow and it was quite chilly. The train station looked like a spider net of railways and people. So many people! I've never seen so many in the same place.

There were hundreds of them and all in a hurry making their own smelly tracks on the big hall floor, or waiting diligently for a train to arrive. Sleeping or reading, eating or just holding tightly their crying babies. Or maybe each other's hands, listening to that thrilling, sensual music flowing smoothly through their own breathing haze. If it wasn't for that music playing the moment I entered the hall room, that moment when I met him…

All that jazz…

I didn't say a thing, I was just quiet. And waited.

It was the first time. The journey. Was it? Yes, it was, so I was both excited and worried at the same time. Everything was new for me; the places, the town, the road. The people. When I think of it I realize that I was so nervous and focused that day that in fact I don't remember much of the trip. Who were those people on the bus, on the train? Don't know. I have no idea. People. Just people. Travelling

People. Like me.

But I did manage to wake up every day since then. Every morning. Today too. And it's a miracle, isn't it?

Where am I? Here, I suppose. Still here, aware of the moment. At least I try. But seen from another perspective, from another side of the Universe, I don't even exist. I am fiction.

How do I look? Still 25

What am I doing? That was a damn good question.

Who am I with?

Well…

I still got the blues

"The Mayans believed in a story in which the universe is born,
but eventually it dies after five thousand years, only to be resurrected
again and again, to repeat the unending cycle of birth and destruction."
(Kaku, M., Parallel Worlds, 4)(Kaku, Parallel Worlds, 2004)

"Could you please spell your name" said the judge.

"J- - A - - ... hmm..." she said, trying to picture the letters. By the middle of the name the judge stopped her.

"Thank you, it's enough", he said realizing she was not used to spelling.

"Whatever" she said to herself, or maybe she only thought of it, letting her hand glide through the air as if measuring the beat of a song.

Unstarted

Unfinished

"Raise your right hand. Place your left hand on the Bible."

She hesitates.

"Ma'am, do you understand me? Do you understand what I'm saying?" said the court officer, raising his voice, looking at the judge with pleading eyes and then with anxiety at the woman standing in front of the desk where two microphones and two copies of the Bible were laying.

She turned her head and looked to the courtroom. Those faces staring back at her, unknown, unwanted. It all felt like a dream, a bad one. It was something that she'd only seen in movies and she never imagined it could happen to her.

"Yes, I understand" she said looking at the court officer who took a few steps towards her to make sure she could hear him.

"Yes, I understand" she repeated, "but I don't believe in God, and I don't believe in the Bible either."

"It's okay! No problem" the judge said. He was a white haired gentle looking old man who seemed more interested in her now.

"Raise your right hand, please" the court officer said.

THE LETTERS

Date: Thu, 15 Oct, 10:07
To: me

The question? We were at the answer... which you failed to give me... regarding the things that you do for your own soul, the things that you feed the maze of your inner self with.

And the question?
9:35
What time is it there?
Ok, but... you didn't answer my question
... So you're not interested in the material aspect of the human existence, most people are – "mea culpa", sorry, but in the spiritual one. Okay.

....

To: me
Interests, hobbies, interpretation of your personal space? Except for your family, your job, your children, presence or absence of pets, and many or not so many miles to the city... what else is there in your life?
Send me a photo
The subject... it's you!
Tell me about yourself

....

You?
You
... Okay. Pick a subject.

....

What a shame. As you wish

....

… Not talking?!...

....

Cool!
Still… not talking?
"Fate"

....

Date: 28/10/ 00:50
From: m

Can I answer your question after you come back?
How long will you be gone? A week?

....

Date: /10/28
You can answer it when you want to, if you want to. I have learned
that nothing is compulsory…
Yes, I'll be gone a week.

....

Date: 31/10/ 10:07
I believed you when you told me you were busy. Should there be any
reason for me not to believe you?

....

Date: /11/1
No, there shouldn't.
I'll be back on Saturday. Till then… you can answer:-))

....

Date: 02/11/ 19:49

Yes master, as you wish. Into deeper water

As you're used to making decisions, which do you prefer: speed-dating, or laid back, relaxed conversation?

....

Date: /11/3
To: m

Both, depending on the situation or your mood. You still haven't told me anything about you.

Are you going to open yourself for me? Just a little bit?

....

Date: 02/11/ 19:24
From: m

If you insist. But I would like you to answer a question first. "You still don't want to talk?"

How did you get to this conclusion? Last time we met, you came to me. We spent the night together in the little room, where you were living at that time, up in the attic. How many secrets we shared that night…

Do you remember?

Was there a time in all these years when you and I happened to meet again, somewhere, by chance or by choice, and I refused to talk to you?

Help me remember

....

3/11/19:24
To: m

We promised each other that no one could ever take away what we had or everything we'd been through together, no matter what may occur later on. I've always had the feeling and the idea that I can hide inside the drawers of my soul the things which are dear to me.

I don't know why but afterwards, I had the impression that you were mad at me. I repeat, I don't know why; maybe I misbehaved or maybe I did some foolish thing, maybe… who knows. Had it been so, I am deeply sorry.

You are special and I've always liked you; I prefer everything to be explained lest there should remain any trace of resentment or sorrows.

I would like to see you again.

Well, tell me about yourself and… help me remember

....

Date: 5/11/ 10:41
From: m

Your silence…
I've opened myself to you. A little bit, just for you. Only now
Is this subject profound enough?

....

Date: 11/5/@:
To: m

I have just written you.

Yesterday I drove for ten hours and I got home late at night. We got caught in a terrible storm. The weather forecast for this week doesn't look promising at all.

You could open yourself up to me… more, just for me, from now on
Yes, I like depths.

....

11/5/?
So, you do remember…
Me

....

11/5/
Reply: to me

I only remember the good things. So I remember

....

Reply | me: to
Now I'm curious. Tell me all about it!

....

Reply | m: to
Generally speaking only good things?

....

11/5/
Reply | to: me

I remember looking at you, in the studio where we used to spend our afternoons

I remember that foggy day when we wandered about and I showed you my favorite places

I remember that time when we went hiking in the mountains.

I remember when we went camping, when we ate crabs.

I remember how we made love

I remember... your taste

....

Sent: Thursday, November 5, 9:47
Reply | me to:

You must be one happy man to remember only the good things. For some reasons, it is said that good things are not remembered so easily while the least pleasant ones willfully persist in our memories.

A self-defense mechanism, probably. Perhaps it is why some people are less communicative. Or not communicative at all. So they can keep all for themselves and unaltered that which they consider to be most precious and valuable.

I don't know if of any relevance to you, but you are the only one who has succeeded in reaching the locked recesses, the most fairly hidden corners of my soul. I have never felt so exposed, so vulnerable, so "naked" as I am now.

Not even when we were making love.

....

Date: November /5
Reply | to: m

You were never exposed, or vulnerable. Not then, and definitely not now.

The only thing you were was open, and you allowed yourself to be looked at, admired, and loved.

When making love, people are overwhelmed by... feelings, sensibility and bliss.

....

November/5/

I remember it too. Every little thing you say.

I also remember the fact that I had no idea, and it seems that I still haven't learned, how to protect my own feelings. I was ignorant of the fact that we should be selfish, that we should carefully weigh each emotion otherwise everything ends up being trampled down, mocked at.

I remember how surprised I was when you went looking for me and I followed you, curious to understand you, hoping that you might care to talk. What surprised me then was the fact that you went searching for me.

In fact I remember...I remember that I want to remember the pleasant things.

I do not know you and you certainly don't know me. It is said that a man becomes interesting after 40, while a woman stays forever at 25. The years that have elapsed have certainly affected us but we don't know how.

Now I remember everything you are telling me. Still I don't remember you telling me anything of the kind back then, or up until now. But you must've had a reason for it. Or more /Me

....

November/6
Reply | to: me

I may have made many mistakes before, I may have even been rude, I may have stumbled now and then, I may have been arrogant at some points...

I've also jumped the gun when it came to a lot of things, and committed rebellious acts as well and I sometimes happened to loosely interpret my moments (!!!) of freedom; I was able to take liberties of all kinds.

We were seeing each other from time to time for the mere reason that I liked you, because I wanted to see you, to have you, to feel you, to know that you were mine.

I used to come back and look for you because I liked you. A LOT!

Please forgive me if I've done something wrong. I did it without being aware of it.

With or without slip ups, with or without confusions, with or without foolish or childish acts,

I have always liked you and...

You must have felt it

You must have realized it

....

November, same Day

I wish I could see you again. I guess I would. Or maybe… I don't know. I don't know how I'd react. Why am I afraid to meet you? I would certainly go along with you and let you decide what came next, just like we did before. Perhaps. I don't know. Now I feel like running away and hiding. In your arms if we were together. I would close my eyes for a minute, and after everything bad would've gone away, and you already told me I'm safe, that no one would ever hurt me again, in that very moment you lift me up, I will talk.

I would have never believed that memories can be so painful. When you wrote me, the intensity with which I relived the moment we met again, frightened me. It shocked me.

Is this what you wanted right from the start?

I thought I knew myself, who I was. But then I began to open myself to you. And in a fit of absence, you invaded me tumbling all my intimacy – thoughts, feelings, memories. Nothing inside me is as it was before. You pulled down my protective wall which I've built ever so carefully and patiently, revealing that you've never actually been out of my life. It becomes obvious that my feelings for you are as strong today as they were then. And it hurts. Physically. Simply and solely. I simply can't shut down my thoughts, I can't chase them away.

There is nothing I can do about it.

I'm defenseless

…..

Reply | to: ME

You are safe

Painful? They are nice memories for me. It is a trip back in time, a dive back into the depth of my soul and sensations. It is a brew of memories, of flavors. It is a vivid album… of our youth.

Yes, if we met I would have probably take your hand and swing you into a timeless rush where I would slowly start to remember everything… while being inside of you.

No, I never had any intention of shocking you. I merely wanted you to be open minded so we could continue one of our conversations started a long time ago.

Fear can be an extraordinary engine. Don't be afraid of fear. It is just another door to an even deeper layer.

I don't want you to feel defenseless. First of all, nothing wrong can happen to you. Secondly you have nothing to lose if you become more intimate with me. And thirdly, I turned forty a few years ago... I have become interesting. ☺

Don't be afraid to let yourself be hunted by thoughts of all kinds. Confront them and your fear will eventually go away. Those are facets of your own personality which you discover only when you expose yourself to a great danger, when you push your limits.

We can never truly know ourselves. Once I spent some time with a person who told me that we were all gifted with 7 eyes which successively open during seven lives but inside we all have the strength and resources to open them all at once right during our first incarnation, if we manage to encompass time with our ambitions and anxiety;

Innocently. Wisely.

Our potential has no limits and may God help us to discover what is hidden deep inside of us, and may God protect us from the entire burden our soul can bear.

Those who have previously passed through our lives have never actually left us. I've known this for a long time. At times I find myself talking to people that I haven't seen in decades. I know I can communicate with them.

It may seem unusual to you but if I open myself up to people, a spiritual connection begins to develop and I end up feeling it physically. I know I have the ability to reach inside fiercely guarded fortresses and touch precious souls.

I know that the two of us have just made love.

Should we meet again it would simply be a matter of putting into practice what has already happened inside our minds and souls.

November/7

You live your life looking to the future but you truly understand its meaning by looking back to the past, someone said.

I've been having trouble sleeping since we started chatting a few days ago. Memories won't leave me alone. Reliving so many years with such intensity in such short time has taken its toll on me. I am unable to concentrate. I can't focus on anything else but the past. But I managed to find out why I remained speechless.

I found out that...

your desire and will have searched for me. And I let you in when you allowed me and I have loved you. Naturally. Intensely. Unconditionally. Without reopening old wounds, without worrying about what would have happened. I learned that you have changed, and you are definitely much more interesting. I learned that I am afraid I might love you.

Again. Unconditionally.

Should we ever meet again, be gentle with me. I beg of you! Unconditionally. Endlessly.

....

November /7
To: me

I have taken your sleep away?

There are still questions left with no answer. Rest your mind at ease. Stop thinking about that.

You are beginning to grasp the true meaning of the great plunge, the taste and the joy of surrendering yourself unconditionally. It feels good. It feels wonderful, isn't it?

I've been mean but only to myself. I have sinned against others all this time being unaware, mad, selfish, arrogant, possessive, proud, jealous, demanding, whatever you may think of but not mean.

Nothing bad can happen to you.

Should we meet again I'll give you what and as much as you want to take from my existence.

With no limits. Unconditionally. Without any regrets and remorse. A parallel time will be opened.

Kiss you…
You can feel it. Can you?

....

November/8
Reply | to: m

No, I am not playing with your peace. It was merely the joy of a reencounter that brought along this tsunami of memories, the experiences as distorted, awkward and childish as they once were and which are now relived inside a mind that is now some years older.
You have nothing to be afraid of.
Take care

....

November/8

Apparently nothing makes sense anymore. I don't think you truly understand. Maybe I should try
to explain it to you.
Do you fear the unknown?
Me

....

Mailed Nov/12
From: me

Have you ever felt that your destiny is different from that of any other person?
When I took my college admissions examination a few years ago I was living with a family somewhere quite far away from the University. I arrived there two days before the beginning of the exams so I did have some time to figure out when and where the exams would take place. I spent the day before the event trying to get some rest and prepare myself for the whole thing. Before lunch I heard the bells from the church

nearby. Curiosity struck me so I immediately went to look the date up in the calendar. Horrified I realized that it was in fact the first day of examination and I had only a few hours left until I was supposed to enter the exam room. It was quite a long road all the way to down town. Eventually I made it to the scene and, oddly enough, there was no one there. For a moment I thought I ended up in wrong place and wanted to leave but the man at the entrance asked me whether I was there for the written exam. He urged me to hurry. Two minutes after I had entered the exam class they shut the doors. In that moment I knew I was going to pass. It was then when my new life began. All alone. In a too big world.

I've spent years haunting this room, searching for answers to questions and desires. To all that surrounded me. I opened windows throwing to passers-by my priceless gifts, making them happy without asking for anything in return. Perhaps I was just expecting a kind word, some gratitude.

For so many years I've watched people passing by and listened to their grief, their desires. Bringing them ease. Their happiness became my own. It brought me joy just to see them happy. I have dedicated myself till the breaking point of exhaustion. And so I began to lose sight of myself. Still I managed to find deep inside of me the strength to fight. To get up and keep going. I found the gates of the room stumbling through the darkness while searching for light. Of some flash of hope that would show me the way. Now I open the gates and leave behind this part of my life. And all I'm taking with me is YOU. Maybe you are my guardian angel or an embodiment of divinity.

Maybe

I have always been aware of the fact that we were living in separate worlds. In different dimensions. You, in immortality and me, just a simple human be. That's why my love was nothing else but love. Unconditional and infinite. Maybe the divinity inside of you was allowed to indulge in sin with a mere mortal. Perhaps I was predestined to fall in love with you a long time ago, to make love to you and keep you locked inside, close to my heart. Our paths have yet again crossed to remind me of you now, after all these years, and to understand that I shouldn't be afraid. That someone is watching over me.

"You are safe!" you said. No one will ever be able to hurt me. You took me into your arms. Lifted me up and loved me. Again. The way only you know how to love a mortal. In your immortal way. I step out into the great unknown that is my life and I'm not afraid for I know you are with me. I believe in the law of physics and mathematics, in chemical and biological processes, but maybe...

Me

....

Date Fri, Nov. 13, at 1:26 PM
Subject: parallel times

I should be rational now.

I guess that we have always lived in parallel times, without really knowing it. The present is only an interfusion of the past with the future. There is no present. Jut memories and desires, which determine the course of our future actions.

That's what I think.

....

Date Mon, Nov. 14, at 12:43 am.
Subject: Influence

Do the things you were told in the past matter all that much now?

For me, all that matters is how you are now; the person that you've turned into in the meantime. And if we ever see each other again, it will be when I'm going to meet an interesting man, with an exceptional emotional intelligence, who knows which sensitive and delicate strings to touch when it comes to a woman; who knows how to love and give, to fulfill undreamt dreams.

I'm fine with just that.

"Be careful!" you said. You don't know me at all. You have no idea what wilderness actually lingers inside of me. It's just waiting to be unleashed and it seems that you are about to do just that. I believe it would've been extremely interesting if the two of us were together. In another place. Or space. Or perhaps time. Maybe a parallel one.

But you still haven't answered me a question. The trapeze artist, when has he ever stopped doing dangerous vaults? Did he want to see how dangerously high and far he could fly while being secured only by the delicate thread of life? Endlessly searching for a new and greater rush every time he felt safe

Me

....

Date Sat. Nov. 14, at 6:21 AM
To: me

Yes. Where would we all be without those who push beyond limits?

Where would we be without the wild and exuberant side that lingers inside each of us?

How could we have ever been able to dream if there hadn't been an Icarus? How would our hopes and dreams of crushing all obstacles ever blossom?

How awfully dull and sad it would be to live without really putting ourselves out there, in the very claws of danger, without breaking the barriers of "reason"...

Right?

My New Path My New Path my new path my new path

Date Sun. Nov. 15, at 3:09 PM

I don't actually know how it will be. Maybe it's already written somewhere. What I do know though, or at least I want to believe I know, is that it won't be as it was up until now.

My new path?

I think I know how I can change things so that they wouldn't be as they were, but I don't really know what the outcome will be in the long run. There are so many things that are impossible to predict. Our meeting for instance. I don't know where my new path will take me now that I've found you again. There are still some things that I can't share with you.

I know what I want. Or not. Maybe not. I am not sure. But I know that in my mind I have created a picture, of how I'd like it all to be. And I wish Reality. To be

Me

....

I was looking up information about someone today. By chance I ended up back to the discussion about parallel worlds between a physicist and a spiritual person, both well-known in their own field of practice. Surprised? No. From their discussion I learned that certain things really are possible.

I wonder if statements are just plain theories.

I believe that each person we encounter, each experience that we go through, no matter how insignificant, may change our lives. All you have to do is to pay attention to the signs that surround you, take hold of them and interpret them according to your own life. You can create in this way the ideal path in the end. But to be able to do such a thing you must be aware of the act itself, of the mechanism that coordinates these fundamental, unwritten, or maybe only by us unknown, laws. And so, eventually, you maybe earn the sense of consciousness through the experience you have gained through the years.

That's why I can't really know what my path will be, since I haven't lived it yet. I wonder what my life would be like if only I had known the few things I know now, from the very beginning.

Would we have met again? Do you think we'll ever see each other again for real? What could we possibly tell each other then?

There's one thing I know for sure. If I'd met you now, in real life, I wouldn't have told you anything of what I had said until now. And of what I may say from now on. Maybe it was meant to be like this. Maybe distance really means safety. And then, what does closeness mean?

Maybe

me

....

Date Mon. Nov. 16, at 1:09 PM

Perhaps, someday I'll tell you why I chose the term "scientific explanations" instead of "possible things". The truth is that things are possible. Am I afraid? No. In fact it's not about fear. It's about trust, about how people would react if they knew the truth.

The Question Is Who Wants to Know the Truth.

I took the risk of trusting you

....

Date Fri. Nov. 20, at 2:13 AM

Forgive me for blaming you for the way my life is. It was unfair of me. You can't prevent someone from falling in love. You already carry the burden of altering and molding other lives. Just the sheer touch of your whispered breath makes me feel as I never felt before

Me

....

Date Mon. Nov. 23, at 2:33 AM

To: me

These past couple days have been pretty busy and tiresome.

I've been in over my head with work. Yes, I like the pieces. I wouldn't display them if I wouldn't like them. I'm the most lashing critic when it comes to my own work.

Perhaps you'll see them one day, right?

Kiss you!

P.S.: Do try and find a piece of jazz entitled "Temptation". I really like jazz. All of my work is born from jazz.

....

Date Wed. Nov. 25, at 1:42 PM

I wish we could meet again. The thought that it will take just as many years until we do see each other again, scares the hell out of me.

"...into deep water..." How could I take such a risk and let myself be carried away to the deepest pits of my soul, forgetting that I can't actually "swim"?

What have I done?

"Take these things as they come and you'll find your peace" you said. It seems that I don't have much of a choice now, do I?

Me

....

Nov. 26, at 2:22 AM

Yesterday afternoon I tried to work but instead I imagined what we would do if you came.

Maybe we would just stay in town, or maybe in its precincts. Or go somewhere else. We would probably have to stop somewhere on the road, at an inn or a hotel. And maybe we would spend the nights together. Maybe we would talk. Or maybe we would keep silent. Me

…..

Date Thu. Nov. @...

I like the imaginings you sent to me. About art. And symbols. How could I resist not

    To Interpret

        If only I could have the power to control feelings and desires, my own thoughts

        Others` thoughts lest my reality should destroy what is innocent and pure

        Unspoiled Dreams.

        Goals

        Love

        Answers

Is this really what we're looking for?

When was the last time you cried?

....

Mon. Nov. 30, at 1:27 PM

To: me

Subject: confessions, explanations

I understand and I respect the depths of the soul because I hope that mine would someday be fully understood, as a whole.

Relax! I'm not misinterpreting you. There are times when I remain silent; it's only because of the chaotic and brutal pace I often work at. It's always been like this. The important thing is that I do communicate; telepathically, spiritually, through vibrations waiting to do it conventionally. Still I read my e-mails every day, and I answer them when I can.

The theory of rational choice…hmm! I think that during my entire life I've made choices that often came from instinct and from heart, based on fear or respect, on the emergency of managing the risks. I've made a lot of mistakes but I've also had a lot of satisfactions. I think that we are too insignificant to put this into an equation. How many times did it happen to all of us to be crazy and prudent and chaotic and gushy… having to bear all the consequences of a choice made in the heat of the moment?

Indeed certain dangerous circumstances have taught me to make a decision quickly like a swift reaction to a specific situation. I probably also fit the profile of an adventurer of time, of an adrenaline addicted pirate or of an emotion kamikaze.

....

Mon. Nov. 30, at 1:23 AM

To my friend

I have to admit you're incredibly gifted. With patience and carefulness you discover, analyze and put together patterns of thoughts, of inner experiences. Then you give them meaning by extrapolating them. You deduce causes and anticipate future forms of an unknown state. You are rational beyond any limit. And that doesn't surprise me. The game you play is extremely dangerous.

Strange, but I never thought that I would ever end up confessing myself, and least of all to you.

You're not the reason for my silence.

In a moment of lucidity I realized I had to break free from this state of emotion and get it together; and just bury myself in work. In two days I have to turn in a paper about the process of decision. In the highest state of irrationality that the shock of our reunion may bring upon me, I had to read and reason about, that's right, rationality. You can only imagine that it was impossible for me to acknowledge what I was reading. I had to be strict and start doing things I didn't feel like doing. I isolated myself. From you.

You're a perfect conversation partner and I miss our little idea-exchange sessions. I miss talking to you. I wanted you to know why I went silent. Again. A little. And if you like, and it's okay with you, I would like to continue our dialogue. Whenever you may want. When there is time, will, desire.

Unconditionally

Until then I will be in my cosmos, contemplating about... rationality

Me

....

Tues. Dec. 1, at 1:37 PM
Reply Forward

I've sent you an e-mail and I hope you liked it. Unfortunately I think I've sent it to another address too. Sorry for that.

....

Date:Dec. 2
To: m

Don't worry! No problem. Even if it did happen, it's not that big of a deal.

Winter's here.

Kiss you.

....

Mon., Dec. 7, at 9:48 AM

Do you remember the time we went to a friend's birthday party, somewhere outside of town? It was summer. We went out in the wheat field and you started sneezing continuously. It was a hot evening and the moon was full.

....

Mon. Dec. 7, at 10:12 AM
To: me

Yes…
I had a lot of things on my mind, back then. Things of you. I've just finished a complicated class; I'm beat. I'm going to wash up and work all night long. I would like to draw a picture of you.
And not only, And not just
And a little more. I invite you to a glass of wine.

Do you feel me?

....

Sat., Dec. 19, at 2:10 PM
To: me
No questions asked. I too have stuff I don't talk about; it's everyone's "right", right?

....

Mon., Dec. 21, at 1:57 PM

It is weird how small things can influence us so much. I've stopped fighting back. But I'd love to understand what's going on and why
Me

....

Sun., Dec. 27, at 1:00 PM

I got the most unusual Christmas gift ever.

I learnt that everything happens for a reason and everything is possible and perfectly plausible

/ me

"Knock, Knock!" "Who's there?"

Sat., Jan. 2, at 8:44 AM

Subject; Focused Intention

"Having an intention is enough to accomplish a result. When properly focused, awareness has the ability to carry out quite specific commands. Every intention is a trigger for transformation. As soon as you decide that you want something, your nervous system responds to reach your desired goal." (Adapted from Ageless Body, Timeless Mind by Deepak Chopra, Three Rivers Press, 1998) (Chopra, Ageless Body, Timeless Mind, 1998)

I remember having fun sometimes…, making a wish to meet a certain person and not long after the wish would come true.

He left and was supposed to call. He didn't. She got worried not knowing what had happened to him. The next day, she took the first train towards the city. She didn't know where to look for him. She thought it impossible to find somebody in the crowd without planning it, and yet, going to that place it seemed the most natural thing at the time. She had gotten there exactly when he came out of the building. She was shocked by the coincidence of the reencounter; but she was still so angry at him for not calling that she no longer focused on the impossible becoming possible.

She went out in the yard to chat with her neighbor. Suddenly, without any explanation what so ever, she turned around and rushed up the stairs. She entered the room the moment the baby was about to fall out of bed. She let the little body gently roll down into her arms.
"Keep dreaming. And smile, little face"

Sat., Jan. 2, at 11:59 AM

"Do you always find answers to your questions?" you asked.

No, I don't. But I'm a terribly curious person. I can't simply accept the fact, the very thing that's happening, without knowing why it's happening. I need to know why, when, how.

I want to know the truth.
And that's

Me

....

What is the soul, actually?
Someone!? Anyone!?
Helloooo....! :-/

And the answer is...

Me

....

Sat., Jan. 2, at 1:48 PM

Okay! So, as you can see, I'm kind of impulsive. Anyway you don't need to worry that I'll pop up at your door step out of the blue, or terrorize you with endless calls

....

Sat., Jan. 2, at 1:52 PM

... and if you still want to draw a picture of me, you can start with my breasts. I really think they'd cover up just about the entire picture.

Obviously, I'm exaggerating a little bit ☺

....

Sun., Jan. 3, at 3:21 AM

I wonder if everything wasn't actually meant to be like this.

If things weren't set beforehand to happen the way they did. Things happen for a certain reason, or so I've heard several times. Or maybe I've just thought about it.

How about you? Have you ever tried to explain why we met?

....

Sun., 3, at 3:58 PM

I wish I knew how many answers a question can hold. Should this situation seem confusing, it's all because of you actually. The effect you have on me. I don't know if I want to meet you anymore. Maybe I fear. The unknown. The absolute chaos. Suspense and unpredictability. Maybe I wish you could understand

Me

....

Wed., 6, at 11:43 AM

I don't know what I was thinking about. In fact there are so many things I think about while reading these lines and trying to grasp their meaning that it's hard to reach a conclusion. About

Me

....

Sun., 17, at 11:37 AM

I have learned that I AM. Illusion. Substance. Definitely &
undeniable, Energy
Me

....

Sun., Jan. 17, at 12:04

I think this is what I have been trying to say all this time but I did
not know how.

My path?

It seems I have to write it with my own hand

Fri., Jan. 29, at 5:37 a.m.

Once a colleague said: "Stop! You're thinking too loud. I can hear your thoughts!"

So unexpected the statement was that I was simply shocked and I could not utter a word for quite a while. When I finally snapped out of it, I realized that in fact it had been all true. That I had heard what I thought I heard. Could it have been possible that I "shared" all the thoughts I had about you, unwillingly and unintentionally?

A thought

What really is a thought? Well a thought is... No. Let's see, imagination is...

Hmmm...

I would like to see the guy that can explain what happens when dreams become reality. When what you want or imagine comes true. It is soul, spirit, voodoo. Nope. Merely science. Physics, mathematics and stuff like that. Biology maybe. Maybe just faith. Too big word. Too Big Word

What a puzzle!

Just playing with

WORDS

What is then the feeling that surrounds me when I think of you? Define. Yes of course, I have to define first.

Words! Phuuu...

....

Wed., Feb. 3, at 1:45 PM

Now I think I have shared everything. With you. Okay, maybe not only you (we are online, right? lol). It was good, wasn't it? I wish I had told you everything right from the start, but I don't know how you would have reacted. And I don't know whether things like sharing thoughts without expressing them, in words (again!:)), are normal or not. Well, you know what I mean.

But what the heck, who is normal now a days?! Maybe. The fool on the hill
(Yes, it's true, I saw him. But this is another story)

....

Wed., Feb. 3, at 7:54 AM

Ever since we were rejoined I have tried to understand what was happening, to find a starting point. And I have realized that nothing from what I experienced so many years ago is so difficult to accept as the feeling of abandonment. Of being defenseless, of being helpless.

It is unbelievable how many things we can find out about ourselves and about others at one point, when truth reveals reality as it is. Naked.

We have not seen each other for years but I sometimes realize that there is indeed a small chance to meet again. Till then

Me

....

Tue., February 9th, at 12:27 AM

I'm going to go on a little trip in April. I think there will be much to see and do. What things or places would you like to see or experience again?

Me

....

Wed., 10th, at 10:37 AM

I will think about everything you've told me and try to get to know you. Again. A little.
In April

....

Mon., March. 1st, at 9:37

I read our e-mails again and much of what you wrote was about this sort of... reality. It's difficult to know how much you have influenced things, or how important you might be, or have been, to the way things may continue to unfold and may be interpreted.

It seems you knew things. How much do you know actually? But you do not have to tell me. Of course it would help me. There have been moments when I thought things were being explained but it's all so complex that all the explanations couldn't have been enough. I don't think that anyone truly knows the reason for everything that happens, and I highly doubt that there is an answer to every question.

It would all be too damn easy.
4

Me

....

Tuesday, March, at 3:28 AM

I've been trying not to think of you, but it's not easy. On that very day, when I sent you that e-mail for your birthday, strange how your name came up in most of the street ads, on TV programs. Even the jazz musician from the corner coffee shop was playing "happy birthday" the same moment I passed it.

I know: coincidences! I should have been used to it. But I'm not.

THE FRIEND

Tue., March 9th, at 12:52 PM

My dear Friend,

You were meant to be involved in this entire story. Perhaps one day I will write down my "memoirs" and you will learn more.

It just so happens that last year I got back in touch with an old acquaintance. I realized that after all these years I was still in love with him. Actually I don't really know what and how it happened. Perhaps things are not as complicated as they appear to be. Maybe I should take them as they come, less tense, and try to "live the moment", as they say. I think that would be best.

I had that inner feeling that I had to tell you about it. I can imagine that telling the one you are in love with that everything you have known about yourself is no longer valid, may seem weird. How would you react to this situation? He remained silent. I would have probably done the same. I don't know. It's difficult to judge people.

I wish you would not avoid me. I'll appreciate more if you tell me what you think. The truth. Well, maybe it's too much to ask.

Who knows the truth?

Me

....

Sun., March 14th, at 3:00 AM

I want to meet someone but I don't know how to find this person. Please don't think I've gone mad when you read about what I am going to tell you about this person.

You know I am not a religious person, that I do not believe in any God and that I have no idea about religion. To be honest, I don't think this person really believes in any god either, but instead he tries to explain certain truths based on a spiritual, a divine perspective. In fact I don't know what he thinks, what he believes in. But I would like to meet him. I think it would be an interesting and unique experience, since spirituality is not easily explained however hard the scientist may try to. But what do I know?

Little
me

....

Anyway, returning to MY muttons…

Being both a physician and a spiritual man (ha, ha, ha! I hope he also has a great sense of humor), I thought that meeting him might be a good idea. To be honest, I do not think he would have the time to meet ordinary people such as myself. I doubt he will. We are all so busy these days. And how would he react if I told him…

How would you react if suddenly someone around you, was thinking too loud, so loud that it bothered you? What if you found out that the person could change your own thoughts?
What would you do?

Do you remember Munch's paining "The Scream"? That is how I sometimes feel. I believe this person is the only one I would dare to openly speak about my nonsense. I think it's all about trust. Maybe he won't find my account all that strange. Maybe my stories would fascinate him, arouse his interest in listening to
The Secrets of a Time Traveler
In mathematical, physical spaces
Cosmic or microcosmic
Or maybe
In mere journeys to Lilliput Land,
The land of ants or Ben's land
Or perhaps the land of the green$
Who knows?
I might be offered a cup of tea with inviting flavors
Magical, oriental
Of the Arabian nights
In emerald palaces, shimmering in rain of sunshine

At the edge of the sea, insurgent and scattered
As the murmur of a starry midnight
Under the wing of a sun torn man

With shadowy lambent glances
Bearer of stardust
The mystery of great secrets
Unfolded in silhouettes of darkened ivory
For who has not forgotten
Spirit, love…
Fiery lust

In the faint hours of a dewy morning
Sipped in an instance
In a sweet whisper
Of divinity
Perhaps
Me

March, 12th, at: 8:37 pm

Subject: speaking of God

Not long ago a guy began calling me at night, by accident maybe. He was sad because his girlfriend had left him. Problems of the heart, you know. The thing is that this guy was calling from another continent, Africa I think. And he was calling me almost every night. He told me about things and the war, about the Desert. If I come to think about it, he was actually nice. When I allowed someone else to pick up the phone, the person changed suddenly his story and said he had been sent by God, or that he was "God's messenger" or something like that, and that he had to call my phone number to discuss this with me. How he came to that conclusion and how he got my number, I have no idea. After all of that, for whatever reason, he never called again

Me

....

Mon., March 15th, at 11:33 AM

Not that long ago, you said that society requires people to behave normally.

In whose name were you speaking when you said that? On your own, others', or mine? I suppose I am part of that society too, am I not? I don't know why you brought up the term "society". Do I owe anyone anything more than I do to myself? And what did you mean by "normal" behavior? What is normal nowadays? What rules should one obey to be considered normal?

Do you remember The Evening Star? You should read it again when you have the time. I've actually reread it and, bit by bit, I began wondering whether the poet had any knowledge of astronomy or cosmology. Although I'm not all that familiar with its theory, the poet's manner of delineating The Evening Star` Metamorphosis reminded me a little of the Big Bang Theory. But he lived in the 1800' s or so. When did this theory appear anyway? I wonder.

I remembered the book on Quantum Physics I had recently bought. I picked it up and opened it precisely at the page where the history of the Big Bang theory was described. Funny, right? I should get used to such sort of things but I am not, and I get a strange feeling every time it happens.

Anyway, the theory was "invented" in the sixties so, even if the poet did benefit from a higher form of education (he studied sociology and psychology among other subjects), knowledge about the Big Bang was practically nonexistent at that time, and certainly not in its current form I presume. I did a Wiki search on the poet and found out that for some time he had been mentally ill and hospitalized for quite some time. I instantly figured that he might have come in contact with his own spirit and perhaps he could have gained a greater understanding of interstellar space. This understanding might have helped him describe the Genesis of the Universe even at that moment, in the 1800's. The problem is that those so called "normal" people, to be read the society, without being able to understand such phenomena, such process, and not having palpable explanation for it at that time, and because of it, society isolated him. To be honest, I've never heard of a psychologist who's gotten in touch with his own spirit and has ever continued to be a psychologist. If you ask me, I think he would've given up on his practice, long ago, and would've tried to find answers that were quite difficult to find.

By the way, do you know who is Psyche? The goddess of the soul who fell in love with Eros and… the story goes on. It's unbelievable how much one can learn from the Internet!
And since we mentioned deities…

SHIVA! I happened to have thought of SHIVA, even though as I previously mentioned, I am an amateur when it comes to religion or gods, or anything like that. Curious as I am I searched for and I found something. It is a deity of love I think, in fact it comes from Buddhism – I am not sure. In any case it has something to do with love. And deities. That is how I gradually found out that the people who connected with the spirit, with psyche, (to be read the psyche), are the ascetic. Those who isolate themselves in sufferance, and abstemiousness. Only meditation. I have never meditated in its denotative meaning but I have thought quite a bit. I like splitting hairs. Why? Perhaps this is me.

This is how I am

Me

p.s. Btw, have you read Larsson's books? Sadly he kicked the bucket. See the movie! There are 3 of them.

....

Mon., March 15th, at 12:02 PM

To: me.
I didn't know. I felt something...

I spoke on behalf of the labeling "masses" which prefer joining the herd, which detest differences, nuances, exceptions...peaks...

We can mention many people that were on the brink of "madness", at least that's how they are seen by the "normal" people, the crowd...while, in fact they were misunderstood visionaries. Kafka, Rousseau, Van Gogh, Bacovia, Luchian, Joyce, Kasey, etc., etc., etc.

Such persons seem to had previously lived and returned to their fellows with feelings, sensibilities and thoughts that were beyond their time, WHICH MADE THEM RESPECTED, BUT MOST OF ALL FEARED, ISOLATED FROM THE REST... LONG MISUNDERSTOOD, LABELED AS BEING FOOLS, TORN FROM REALITY...

I have read the books; I like to visualize the atmosphere.

Don't give me any details; everybody weaves their existence as they see fit, as they can, as their courage guides them to (re)direct it, as they feel, don't they?

I would respect intimate moments and experiences, dreams and hopes, desires and recesses for respect itself, for freedom BUT MAINLY BECAUSE I EXPECT MINE TO BE LIKEWISE RESPECTED AND UNDERSTOOD IN RETURN!!! Or at least accepted.

The soul opens up when the grounds are set, when the clock strikes, when the tongues of the mind are untied. I don't think it can be anticipated or programmed. It just happens and…we almost become the actors-victims of our own emotions in resonance with the stars. That's what I think.

....

Wed., March 17th, at 11:46 AM

Subject: a thought experiment

"Without consciousness acting as an observer and interpreter, everything would exist only as pure potential. That pure potential is the virtual domain. It is nonlocal and can't be depleted; it is unending and all-encompassing.

Tapping into that potential is what allows us to make miracles." (Adapted from Power, Freedom and Grace by Deepak Chopra, Amber-Allen Publishing Inc., 2006)(Chopra, Power, Freedom and Grace, 2006)

Hi! Have you had the chance to look into what I asked you? About Guru? I think he lives somewhere in C. I am going to try to find a scholarship for a summer class but not for this summer, I don't have the time. Maybe later.

I told you I have taken up classes of yoga. Last time I was there I realized that the person at the reception desk knew a lot of stuff about me. I could never understand how that was possible. Perhaps it was just a coincidence. In any case the advice I got was helpful, thus very welcomed.

"Great then!" anyone would say. "You have no reason to complain". Except it is not hard to become paranoid when your life is a continuous string of weird coincidences and what you think of at a certain moment comes true the next second, and bits of what you are experiencing every day, a part of your life, perfectly match with what you are experiencing in a different space, the very next, as in a parallel world.

I wish I would meet him but I am afraid. For so long no one has touched me. I dream of making love. I long for it but I don't know how I will react, overcome by so much emotion, by feelings and desires. What real or unreal world will we reach?

You, what would you do?

....

Fri., March 19th, at 1:17 PM

How do you get along with your girlfriend? You were saying you wanted to lose weight.

If you want a recipe to losing weight and don't want to get a dog and have to walk it early in the morning and late at night, then I suggest you should fall in love. Head over heels, if possible.

Look at me! I went from a size M to a S. How nice, right. I should get this guy to buy me some new clothes now that everything is way too loose. Luckily I don't have time to go anywhere because I have too much to do. This morning I had to submit a paper with a deadline at 11 am. It was an awful course. Had I known it, I would have chosen another one. Its' content was interesting but the lecturer was beyond help.

The difference between this course and the rest is like the difference between f...* and "make love" (excuse my colloquial speech). First one you have more or less for pleasure, the second one, for passion. It doesn't mean I have such outstanding experience in the field.Sogetcrazy in love! I really recommend it!

Do you know that in fact the expression "crazy in love" comes from a pathological state? That is why it is called "crazy" because the behavior is similar with such pathology: you can't sleep, you can't eat, and you are constantly thinking about him/her, you have stomach aches. I haven't had a decent meal since having rejoined with him. Will there be... 5 months?! And when thinking about my upcoming trip, of all the goodies from there... and I will just be staring blankly at. It's not funny, but I am a size, almost, XS now! Not bad, not bad at all. Maybe I should thank him after all.

But I digress. Let's talk about sex.

The researchers found out that during sex, at the moment of climax, only one area is activated in the male's brain, the "reward center" for a well done job, while the female brain remains "silent". Quite interesting. The woman seems to be much more profound at the moment of climax than a man. It appears to be linked to the process of procreation. Or affection.

Never show too much girl!

....

The train was crowded that day. The man, wearing a yellow turban, offered her the seat by the window. She kept on thinking, being in her own world, musing about spirituality, about nonlocal, about...

"You are already a spiritual entity" she heard. She looked at the man sitting next to her, at his image reflected in the window. His eyes were closed and his face calm. He looked as he was meditating.

This world is very interesting when it comes to soul and spirit. It is a world of silence, of safety. Of experiences, and surprises. As a matter of fact I am not sorry about what I am living now, and I do not care what people say about me. I wish they could experience it too.

She remembered that day when one of her friends had asked her if she could stop thinking too loud, as if he had heard her thoughts.

"This is what I get if I think too much. I thought it was only when talking too much, people are being irritating"

The previous day she had wondered what it would be if someone could hear what others were thinking about.

"It could be interesting. Cool, exciting. And funny. Think! You can say exactly what you want, curse anyone as much as you like and still look innocent as no one would know where the thought came from."

And then she found out that one of her friends, originally from Bangladesh or so, regularly practiced meditation. Not so strange that he could hear her thoughts.

She felt happy.

....

The door of the subway train was about to be closed.

"That young girl, is she going to make it? Come on, hurry up! You can make it" she said to herself.

"If I only was a little bit closer to the door … Just to stretch my arm and pull her in" she thought.

Within a second the lady in front of her, stretched her arm and pulled the young lady onto the train before it started moving.

....

Sun., March 21st*, at 5:23 AM*

Hi!

Is your brain in pain while reading what I wrote to you?! How do you think I feel?

A while ago I had posted a picture online. Nothing out of the usual. The interesting thing was that all the people who I chatted with that day, had something to say about it. It doesn't matter what they said but all the chats were a general "answer" to my question what did they think about that picture. I was surprised and I did not understand how there could be so many people, living so far away from each other, that could react in the same way as an answer to a question I had not expressed verbally.

And then I thought about the existence of a net of relationships, of the fact that the universe is synchronistic and coincidental. And that everything is connected with everything else. Should we be in synch with the universe, does it mean that what we experience is synchronicity? The more connected we are, the more we experience coincidences or simultaneous event.

Not long ago I called him. I had to hear his voice, to feel him. I needed a bit of reality.

"Are you going to travel back home?"

"Maybe, I don't know".

There was a moment of silence, and then he continued:

"I will know soon. Maybe" he said. Then a short break.

"Unless you come and I see you, what's the point of this trip?" she thought.

"Maybe we will see each other" he said.

"Yes, maybe" she answered and closed her eyes.

March

That thing, about thoughts, you know…

You ask a question and then shortly you get the answer, whether expectedly or unexpectedly, it's less important. The important thing is the fact that you are given an answer. And this is even more difficult to explain when other people are involved.

How are thoughts correlated?

Our phone conversation was special as if he had been the only one who answered intuiting my thoughts, as if he had heard and understood them. In fact it wasn't even a question. It was an intense experience, full of desire, expectations and the unknown. Had he felt my inner mood and thoughts?

It's so cool! To observe that I was asking a question and sooner or later I received an answer. I don't know exactly how, but it is exactly that sudden happening which can make life become charming, magical and unpredictable.

…………………………………………………………………………………………

One of the colleagues helped me once and I wanted to thank her. She had left shortly before I did, and I had not realized it until later. I thought that perhaps I could catch her so I hurried. I had hardly reached the entrance to the subway when my colleague was just making her way out of a nearby shop. Was it just coincidence?

The question is, and I'm asking myself, what forces of your thought (?!) are enabling another person's action, to be delayed. If that is indeed what happens. Maybe it was not so strange that she went into the shop but the fact she came out exactly when I was in front of it.

Her friend lived nearby, though she was not sure exactly where. She had been there before but it was a long time ago. She walked around for a while hoping she would remember the place. "It's impossible to find something when everything looks the same" she thought and looked at the row of houses painted all in the same faded red color. The next moment a flash where her friend was sitting at the table, made her stop. "Look at the windows!" she heard the thought.

At the third house at the kitchen table leafing through a magazine was her friend with a cup in his hand, unaware of the unexpected visit.

And I wanted to go to my class reunion. What on earth would I tell my colleagues when they ask what I have been doing?

"Well, you know, here and there. Curbing some spaces, changing some time. Everyday day stuff, you know. What people do"

And what would they say?

"She's really gone "bonkers" hasn't she? Poor thing!"

"Yes, yes, but at a quantum level", I should argue.

I've looked for that movie "Radio man" that you told me about, but couldn't find it.

How new is it?

Me

....

Tue., March 23rd, at 1:57 AM

You told me to stop thinking too much.

"The more connected we are, the more we experience coincidental or simultaneous events. Therefore never ignore coincidences." (Adapted from Power, Freedom and Grace by Deepak Chopra, Amber-Allen Publishing Inc., 2006)

Long ago I have met someone. Somewhere. The following summer I went to visit an acquaintance. There were a lot of people as usually during the season, walking around doing nothing. Just living. There are moments when you don't really know what you would like to do, have no plans. No ideas. And is like it doesn't matter so much what your next step is. Just let it happen and follow the stream. One of those evenings I walked into a boutique at the same moment another person was walking out of it. Not long after that, the same person came up to me and started a conversation. It was he, the friend I had met a few months earlier. He had told me about the plans to visit the place but we had never talked about it in detail. We hadn't been keeping in touch.

How is it possible for two people to be in the exact same place at the same time in a "sea" (cliché, I know) of people without planning it?!!! Yes, I was shocked. I don't know if I will ever truly understand what is actually happening.

What forces drive space and time to converge and intersect?

"Stop thinking so much!" you said.

It was one of those boring days when you have to travel but you rather would stay in bed, nice and cozy, waiting five more minutes. Just five more minutes until it's time for brunch.

The train was crowded and I was close enough to hear the conversation in front of me. I was awake, almost. I think. And they were talking, and talking. And just kept talking. God how they were talking! Don't people have better things to do on the train? Well they are very young and don't seem to be from here. Where could they come from? If I only could open my eyes more and take a look and... A few seconds later that 'big mouth" guy started telling his friends that he was from the South, he lived in a big city with his sister and that he came here for his studies. Okay, now I know. I can go back and try to sleeeep a few more minutes. Great! I just have to ask a question and... I could have stayed in bed longer. No one would have noticed my presence. Hmmm, I mean absence. Whatever. And since I can get the answers just by thinking the questions, than why do I have to travel to be there? Because you have to interfere with The REALITY, idiot!

Well, that might be a plausible answer. I agree.

How can one be so tired?

I actually don't know what to think of what is happening. It seems it is possible to intervene in the course of events in such a way so you can get what you want. By wanting to know where the guy came from, maybe I didn't only anticipate what they were going to talk about. Maybe I "just" influenced the course of their discussion because I was soooo tired and wanted to sleep and was grouchy and really wanted to know where they came from so I could tell them to stop talking so much. So I could take it easy, relax and… well, I suppose now it was too late to sleep but you understand what I mean.

You told me to stop thinking so much. Will I be able to understand a bit of quantum physics just by thinking about it, it would be AWSOME! Maybe I should have a little "talk" with the mathematician as well not only with my guru.

Talking about Guru, where the h*** is he? I wrote to him that I had "a time-space issue" but I don't think he believed me. I don't think he even read what I wrote. Perhaps he has his own soul to deal with, who knows. LOL!!!

....

Did you know for instance that somewhere in the brain there are centers responsible for different activities such as visualizing objects and occurrences? This center can become so excited that is almost impossible for the person to break away from images. Someone told me once that there are experiments in which the subjects are put in extreme circumstances without food or water, but mostly without getting any sleep or rest. It was about situations of fear, insecurity and anguish, to see how the subjects' mind reacts.

One of the days I sent a friend a book as a birthday present. It was about physics and parallel worlds, stuff like that you know. I wasn't sure about the address so I didn't know what to do. He had been gone for a while but guess what? He received the book personally a few minutes after he returned home. Great, isn't it?! Maybe it was that "real-unreal" thing, the soul, my soul of course, that kept an eye on the whole thing to make sure that the book will arrive just in time.

If I only knew how this trick works and I had a penny for each time things like these happen to me… Wow! How rich I would be! Maybe
I AM

Me

....

March, same year

"And smile when watching the stars."
Do you remember?

"Do not be afraid to be afraid" He told me. It is actually a statement which invalidates itself. Therefore fear should not be considered as fear with its usual meaning, but as an epiphany. As an experience that opens doors for knowledge and self-knowledge. It brings a redefinition of the soul from a different perspective. From a different existential dimension.

"You are safe" he said. "There is nothing to fear, if you get closer to me." And I did. Perhaps that is what helped me. I got closer. "You give me too much credit" he also said but maybe he does not know things about himself either. What forces lay in him. In us. Maybe he is the embodied divinity. The Guardian Angel

Oh my god, Impetus. Not this word again. Excuse my ignorance, I promise I'm ashamed. 5 minutes. But I couldn't find it in any dictionaries so explain it, or I'm not going to sleep tonight. Please, please, please! / Me

. . . .

23 March, at 10:58 PM

From: newsletter@californiasunset.de

To: my friend

Not so long ago I was thinking what it would be like if… Actually I pictured us all alone on a beach, somewhere on an island. We were making love under the starlit sky. The day after, I received an email. I think it was from a record company I used to subscribe to. New Waves Music or something like that. I don't really remember the name. Great music! Blues and Jazz.

And it said: "Friends of perfection! When, I ask you, was the last time you served your lover a dry Martini on the rocks, while in the attic you can hear the brass swinging? And when, I ask you, have you last made love under an incandescent starlit sky?"

Have no idea how is it possible to get this email so soon after imagining something that I never experienced before. A dream, a thought or whatever it was. A vision? Maybe you can explain it because I can't. I wish the wish to come true. But the thought, or the vision...

May a thought come true?

Me

....

Wed., Mar. 24, at 1:21 PM

Impetus, please!
Or else I will not be able to sleep.

Grammar and some technology

Fri., Mar. 26, at 2:02 AM

"You have to remember!" I told myself, and I started writing.
I put "IS" between quotation marks.

Apparently how we speak is important. Yes of course it's important, everyone knows it but what I am referring to is a series of very interesting experiences I had which made me pay more attention to the way we express ourselves. After reading about grammar I started to wonder if not what was going on around us was rather a consequence of the grammatical tenses we use in our conversations than a result of our conscious, should I call it, rational behavior.

It seems that the way a text is written, the grammatical tenses and the information contained and presented in the text, have a huge impact on the manner in which the text is read, perceived and consequently on the concatenation of events.

Not long ago I had a wish, that I would like to go on a trip at the seaside and being there that I would like to stay in the old town. There are so many mysteries and stories in such a place, an old town. And all you have to do is to open your eyes. And mind. Okay, your soul too. Or was it about the mind? To open your mind and to be open minded. That sounds better, since I have no idea what the soul is. I've actually got that trip and I've also got the place. Guess where? In the old town J

I like both old and new, modern cities but I like most the old ones. In fact I like buildings, houses. Big, small, grey, colorful, simple, sophisticated, futuristic or ancient. I was even thinking to write a book about a city. A big city, a metropolis, so old that it has become modern. Edgy. If you look at the sky, it's all you can see. The sky edgy.

I am babbling too much. I should stay on topic because I have a lot of work to do and in a week I am going on holidays. I know you will say that it would be very difficult to truly explain these sorts of things. I find it strange how thoughts appear and disappear in certain situations, when people are close for instance. Sometimes too close. But who cares? Me of course, otherwise I wouldn't terrorize you with my "hocus-pocus"- letters.

....

March, 27, no idea what the time was

Subject: about technology

TV is a very interesting technological invention. Sometimes I am under the impression that I have my own private broadcasting.

A while ago I was speaking with a friend about spending New Year's Eve overseas. I was not very convinced about this idea because I didn't know what the city was like during winter. Cold and icy with mountains of snow along the streets impossible to come through, always in chase to find a free place at the window in a coffee shop to warm up frozen fingers and toes. Luckily I didn't have to keep on asking "what if", and "how" and stuff like that because that same evening on the late night show images of the city during winter were presented. So it had been enough to ask the question for the answer to come shortly after that. How cool is that?!

I must say I had quite an interesting week. I managed to get stomach problems amongst others and I threw up an entire night as if it wasn't enough that I had lost so much weight that all my clothes were too big for me. I am only breasts. Brains, breasts and the (not) holy spirit in my case. Btw (which is the short term for "by the way" but I know you knew that), If you need a subject to think of :). Please tell me if I am boring you with my chat. Anyway, I needed two days to recover.

Why am I telling you all these things? (About writing or about losing weight you should ask now because this is what I am doing right now, asking myself. I believe it's about writing definitely. And losing weight. Why not? In fact I have to admit that I feel quite comfortable like this, smaller). So that it won't happen again like it did last time, many years ago. I should have taken notes then too and maybe changed the history. My history of course.

It's a good idea to take notes. Think of how many ideas are, or could be, born every second just you pay enough attention to your being! You could easily fill a whole notebook in a day. And then sell the ideas. It is not a bad idea. Repetition! Is not so "chique", I know. Not when writing but sometimes Repetitio Es Mater Studiorum! As the Latins used to say if I come to think about it.

We have a flower, a lily. Last time it blossomed was seven years ago. Last week I thought I should throw it away. The next day a bud appeared and now it is in full blossom. Do you think the lily heard my thought?

Me

....

Sun., Mar. 28, at 2:44 AM

"Think about what happiness means to you!" the text said.

"Imagine, visualize a moment in the future when you are happy, cherish this moment and let it influence your life" one of gurus texts said (I told you about guru and his texts, didn't I? They are interesting. I am just wondering who the real author of these writings is). I did and the result was that, and I am not going to give you the details because this time I want to keep them for myself, in the next issues of my crosswords magazine, one of the articles describes my wish as I imagined it. It even had a photo, not with me of course but pretty much as I had it on my mind. The image of what happiness would mean to me.

Finally
Last evening, actually the whole day yesterday, I sat at the computer writing an application. Late at night when I thought I reached the end of the application I pressed a button and part of it disappeared. Nice, isn't it? How much fun a computer can be! And how many "nice" words you remember from time to time.
Technology!

M

....

March, at: 2:45

Have I told you about my trip to Paris a few years ago? Don't think so. That was something to remember, I can assure you.

I arrived at the station late in the afternoon and went on the first street with the intention of finding a map of Paris and a hotel. I stepped into the first hotel I found and asked them politely if they had a good map of Paris and if they could recommend a nice hotel. "Totally and completely foolish!" as they use to say. I think they were shocked or they thought I was joking. Or stupid. Or both. Obviously they offered me a very good price to stay at their hotel. This is what happens when you let people like me, crazy people. Loose. How else can I put it?

Absolutely clueless and foolish one should say. But this is how I am. A dreamer.

Not that bad!

It was a thin, warm rain and the boulevard was so crowded that I could hardly walk. I was wondering if it wasn't a better idea to continue on the other side when I saw this little old man cross the street and walk straight towards me. He asked if he could walk with me and began to talk. About the city, about places. "How strange" I thought, "why did he stop exactly in front of me and start to talk to me as if we knew each other?" We continued to walk in the crowd and it didn't bother me anymore. Without noticing it we became a part of it and we were just following the wave. Without wondering or questioning it.

He started to tell about times long before I was born. About the concentration camp during the war, about the time he spent there. I said no word, just listened. When we stopped I realized we were in Montmartre. That is where I had actually planned to go but I didn't know the way.

....

Still March

I sneezed. So beautiful and romantic spring is(unless you don't have to sneeze fifteen times in a row)! One day I will tell you how important a sneeze is. What about a kiss in a field of wheat, on a warm summer evening with a full moon? Summer? Yes, definitely. Wheat field? No, no wheat fields but strawberry fields. Forever! Sounds better, feels better too. And perhaps a glass of wine. Red.

When I come to think about it I realize I haven't drunk wine for a long time. And my friend said he would teach me how to drink and then I'll know his language by heart, he said. Ha! I would like to see that. I actually tried to learn that language so many times but for some reason I have never managed to do more than the introductory class. And I was pretty good. I think I should make an effort and start learning it again. Language rules, grammar rules. But what am I going to do about guru, about micro and macro universes? About that damn psyche (meaning mine) and the "unholy" spirit (that's mine too)? Because some are like that, they have a less "holy" spirit.

"Come on, you are starting to get crazy again!" is what you might say now, but taking into consideration that we have known each other for so many years now, my dear friend, I think you could expect anything from me.

I am so lucky we are not living in the Middle Ages or else they would have burnt me by at the stake a long time ago like that poor Bruno.

But the ones burnt at the stake were the smartest, right (remains to be seen if there is something smart about letting yourself to be burnt at the stake)? Hmmm, I think I meant to say wise but this is not the right word either. Anyway they must have strongly believed in their ideas if they were able to sacrifice their lives for the sake of the truth. How smart is that? To sacrifice yourself. Need I say more?

Have a good day
Or night
Or dawn
Or twilight,
Or
:)
Me

....

Mon., Mar. 29, at 3:22 AM

To: me

I have barely touched the laptop because we are extremely busy the whole day. I don't even have time to breathe. I will be home soon. On May I am leaving to A

Ordinary days from an ordinary person's life

Sun., Apr. 4, at 12:31 PM

"Spirit is not verbal like other thoughts in your head. It comes as insight, an "aha!" that makes you see things in a new light. Spirit doesn't argue or try to persuade. It shows you what is real in a given situation, pure and simple" (Adapted after Deepak Chopra)

Tomorrow I am leaving on vacation. I don't know what it will be like. Hopefully fine, but it remains to be seen. On the way back home I have planned to visit the old part of the city where unfortunately I'll be for a day only. Maybe the weather will be on my side.

Yesterday, while talking about the trip, I turned on the TV and there was a show about the old town. Great, isn't it?

The other week I had to meet a friend so I took the train. On the way, without any apparent reason, I remembered things that had happened before when several times I happened to get off the train in the exact place where the person I was supposed to meet was standing. Even this time the person was standing on the platform exactly where I had descended, as if we had agreed on that.

Do you know what quantum mechanics is? A few days ago I received an email with an attachment explaining it briefly. It is like being in three places simultaneously but at the same time in none of them. It is as easy as that! Therefore make a wish, think of something, and it will come true. Talking about quantum or parallel worlds or...

What on earth am I talking about?

maybe

These Days, 5:17am

I don't really know what he (my friend) believes in. He obviously thanked me for the book I sent him and said he would actually try to read it, not just browse through it.

But I know he is a kind person and a gentleman and that he would have never told me that he didn't like the book or that he didn't believe in these types of things. Physics and quantum and stuff like that. In fact I made the same mistake as that person who had sent me the Easter emails, a little bit different from my beliefs if I can put it in this way. I do hope that one day he will let me know his honest opinion about what he believes.

When talking about God, as far as I'm concerned "I won't believe it until I see it!"
"Every man has his hobby-horse!" Some, like me, have a lot. In fact I don't know why I am telling you all this. Apropos of hobby-horses some have a lot, as I said.
If we ever happen to meet again, and if you happen to give me a hug, a kiss, completely innocent and unconditionally
then

....

Wed., Apr. 14, at 6:10 AM

I got out of the bed, pulled the window curtain aside and looked outside. There was a blue car stopped across the street. Then a white car crossed the street.
Have you known that blue is the color of the soul and white represents purity? I found it out when I went to one of the art museums. The artist, a famous ?, had used in his paintings blue for the soul. His soul. I don't really know if there is a certain way of interpreting life and I am not sure that I understood how he interpreted it. Maybe he went about it in the same way, observing. He looked at what was happening around him, he listened and noticed details that at a first glance seemed trivial then pictured it in its own way. A traffic sign, a text read in a rush. A flower. An open window. A child. A face. A smile.

Do you know how many combinations could be made of three letters and three numbers? Poems could be made if you wanted to. All variations are accepted without exception. This is what I call creativity.

She was on the way to the airport. Everything was flowing and so did her thoughts, in a coherent and meaningful flow, until the eyes stopped on an enormous text with huge letters: PARADISE. It was like a natural extension of the thought she had had at that moment.

Something completely normal maybe, as an answer for what had been the question not so long ago.

....

Wed., Apr. 14, at 8:40 AM

Subject: Don't interfere with the flow

"There is a profound Buddhist doctrine that speaks of a great river that flows through all of reality. Once you have found yourself, there is no more cause for action. The river picks you up and carries you along forever after..." (Adapted from Reinventing the Body, Resurrecting the Soul, by Deepak Chopra, Harmony Books, 2009)(Chopra, Reinventing the Body, Resurecting the Soul, 2009)

It was totally unexpected to suddenly be in an environment as spectacular and fluid as the Sea. The feeling was so powerful that I ceased to exist. I disappeared somewhere in space and only the thought was left.
During the night I had a dream.
"What is it like in paradise?"
"The Earth is paradise" the answer came, and I kept on dreaming.

The train was approaching the final station. Through the window she could see the silhouette of the old town. She started to think about what happened during the day; the museum, the people and all the coincidences. She looked at the text on the computer screen hanging above the benches and started reading quickly parts of it, apparently without any connection. Then the word "color" appeared on one of the buildings, covering most of it.

"So that I wouldn't forget about the sunset" *she thought and watched the Sun disappear silently.*

I strolled through the old town and I loved it. At first I followed the map then I let the destiny lead me. I let things happen. I walked around without knowing where I was or where I should go next. It was amazing how each time I ended up in the place, I imagined minutes before. Of course I never bought a thing of those I imagined. Things didn't matter anymore. It was the magic that was important. And I was playing with it. It was a game of thoughts and strings and micro – multi universes. It was cool and fun and joyful. And happy. I was free

April 20, at noon

I should have told you more but I didn't want to. I didn't tell you everything. I didn't tell you all my thoughts because it would be impossible. Maybe one day you will learn what it was about. But tell me, who would want to meet a freak like me, an anomaly?

Perhaps the best thing would be to start writing down my "memoires" and stop bothering you with my emails. And these boobies of mine, what a pain! As if it wasn't enough, exactly in this very moment the computer "snapped" and made me jump up from my chair. What on earth is wrong with this computer? I did make sure that everything was okay.

Me

....

April 20th, it should be pm.

Subject: apropos of technology

I think I have told you about those crazy electronic things and the thoughts on the fixation we seem to have with high tech nowadays, on all the junk and machines around us. And all is about technology today. And tomorrow. And in order to know how to use them you need to educate yourself as if you couldn't live without them. Yep, that's true. A bit difficult when coming to high tech and special math and nano, and multiverses, and multi-dimensional reality but what the heck, we have plenty of time and nothing more interesting or important to do, since everything is depending on I. T. . . .or E.T

I pressed the button again; I shouldn't have for sure. Some sort of safety button. I'm nearly afraid to breathe when I am sitting at the computer, trying to be creative.

I forget about creativity, about him, about missing him. I could even strongly argue that I forget about everything and everyone when technology is not working. And then, when you can't find what you have written... That is another problem, as you have to conjure all the gods but firstly all the saints from around, and swear that you will not touch anything else but those buttons with funny signs called letters. And then you rush to find the number of the company responsible for making the product and you hope and pray that you'll speak your own language because you never know in which part of this world are the ones answering the phone.

And while you spend the time trying to recover well hidden files on that thing called PC, and you pray (if you haven't done it yet you will do it now, and if you don't know how you will learn it pretty quick) you realize by the unusual tired accent at the other end of the line that they haven't been able to wake up yet as it is midnight there. Good luck with that!

But I think we were talking about my boobies. And about the P.C. Exactly!

What is wrong with this pc, as we have just talked about technology? I hope it won't break down. Sometimes it infuriates me but otherwise we have a good collaboration, really pleasant in fact. Most of the time. And it is helpful. Let's be serious and admit the truth. How else would you keep in touch if one is here another one is there up close or far away if not by using the technology? My dear technology. This is how things stand with "someone up there, in cyber space, loves you".

The other day I was thinking about my friends "up there" and while sitting at the table my eyes fell on a t-shirt with a super modern pc print saying "we are superlative conspiracy" They pick all sorts of texts now days. What did they mean by it? They cashed the money for the t-shirt, that's for sure.

How good of a friend are you with your computer?

....

She had cooked porridge. Suddenly the thought took her to the young girl. Maybe she hadn't eaten yet. So she prepared another serving. When the food was ready, the front door opened.
"Are you hungry?" she asked her.
"Yes!"
They ate in silence. The young girl had been really hungry.

....

She listened to his breath, to the rhythmical beats of his heart. It was so soothing. They had made love and now they were resting. The room was bright, full of warmth and serenity. Suddenly the door opened and the person came in. In reality

She turned her head towards the clock on the wall.
It was 3 pm.

....

Thu., Apr. 22, at 8:00 AM

"Don't interfere with the flow", she read.

This flow, is it informational flow or what? Definitely informational flow. It should be. We are breathing, eating, sleeping, and even peeing information. You have to be a good informational swimmer otherwise you drown pretty quickly in truth and lies. That's information too.

Or could it be that network of relationships Guru was talking about?

Rereading these lines and looking back in time everything seemed so simple, so easy to explain. She lay down on the bed to get some rest. Closed her eyes waiting for sleep to come and imagined she was somewhere far away, on a sunny beach with waves bathing the sun. A lagoon unhampered by anyone. She would swim. She would allow the sun heat to run through her body and to warm her.

She would listen to music.

Jazz

Fishes in a Bowl

Is there a soul?

How was that Greek thing? "Dubito ergo cogito, cogito ergo sum". Or was it Latin? It doesn't sound as Greek to me so it has to be Latin. Definitely Latin! Forget it! It was Descartes. René Descartes, actually. French. Yes, a French philosopher, mathematician and writer and no way that was in French because I know French. It was in Latin. Mmm… Internet… Will never nag again about online surfing (yes, it's Simpson talking right now. Stupid TV!).

But let's not forget the beginning.

I have to admit, the assertion about parallel universes is not only interesting but fascinating. Should these parallel worlds exist, they would probably be equal in terms of space and time.

The next moment a red light slowly appeared on the ceiling. Then red, blue, white, silver and then gold. She closed her eyes trying not to think about anything and especially not about parallel worlds. Even if the idea of parallel existences took her imagination into unreal spaces and times, letting her playing with dreams and thoughts and questions like "what if", she thought it was too complicated to understand it. A feeling of warmth and relaxation filled her body then everything became blurry. Images passed her mind so quickly that she could hardly decipher something. Lines, voices and shades, everything mixed altogether forming complicated pattern of strings.

The noise was almost imperceptible but loud enough to make her startle. "So much for sleep" she thought and went to the kitchen. The recipe book was on the table. There was not so much to do but to wait few more hours until it would get completely dark and try to sleep again. She did as she always does and just let the book open randomly. A phone company advertised major discounts. Then she started read, unable to control what she was reading.

There were words from the recipe on the same page: He, almond, comes, together (?!) fast, beautiful and others.

"What the heck is this? An advertising company in a recipe book! And why did He appear again in the story?"

Considering these small and totally insignificant events of my everyday life, I could say a series of happenings I have experienced might be explained. Why is it that I'm getting answers to my questions? That's funny because it seems I have no answer to this question. Now that I'm writing it all down I can see I was right all along. Now I can see that... In fact I have no idea how or what I was right about. I really need to make research in the domain. Of the soul. In the true acceptance of the word.

What strange weather! In the morning it was snowing and now the sun is shining and warming everything. There are no clouds. I would dare to say it is spring already but you never know here. Perhaps it won't be long until spring, after all

Me

· ·

Sat., Apr. 24, at 5:17 AM

Last night I started watching a B movie. I had nothing better to do and I was really tired but the movie was soooo awful bad that I didn't want to miss it. It was about a young super tuff woman, size zero of course because they can't afford to eat, only once a week, and fantastically beautiful of course, because it's only these girls that are fantastic and super tuff, who had extra-sensorial abilities with the power to foresee future events. Of course. The "A" secret organization, you know the type of organization you have it in all B movies of course (yes, I know- repetition, but Repetitio est mater studiorum as our beloved Latin used to say), made experiments with her subconscious, of course, while her friends were trying to protect her. Did I mention of course? Yes of course! Lol

Of Course a series of events more or less unusual (read ridiculous) occur, keeping the audience (that's me!) under pressure (to keep the eyes open probably) bla, bla, bla, and guessing. The idea of the movie was to use the super-duper Photoshoped powder-puff girlie/ woman to create a powerful weapon to control the world bla, bla, bla, and to keep idiots, as I, up late in night instead of getting a good night sleep and be fresh and handsome and tip-top for the next day. I think it is the coffee talking now. I swear! Nothing else but coffee. Soon awake.

As I said the theme wasn't new but they had however managed to make a movie out of it and got enough "botherless" people to follow it (is botherless a word? Yippee! I finally made my contribution to the world).

Speaking of nothing, do you know what I found in one of the articles online? Damasio, a researcher or so, wrote that "emotions and consciousness are also vital to the higher reaches of distinctively human intelligence. Contrary to some popular notions emotions do not "get in the way" of rational thinking - emotions are essential to rationality" (Damasio, A., Review of The Feeling of What Happens: Body, Emotion and the Making of Consciousness).(Damasio, 1999)

Great guy this Damasio! I like him. After all it is not so crazy what he says. When I think about the events of the past and after I read and reread texts, I somehow understand perhaps not the cause to its full extent but at least the effect of some causes. I don't believe there was something unusual. Rather something normal and mundane, something that belonged to the ordinary. Perhaps it was the Magic. Some would say maybe the imaginary. The cultural or the occult? Or maybe the scientific. Or the science-fiction. All in parallel Worlds

Do you like smoothies?
You should try raspberries, yogurt, banana, dark chocolate (at least 80 % cocoa), Goji berries and maybe almond. And cinnamon. Absolutely cinnamon.

Bon appetite, Mon Ami!

Me

Tue., Apr. 27, at 12:03 AM

I have told you I had taken up yoga classes, haven't I? I had a beginner's manual. I did all the exercises just by holding the book in one hand. Can you believe it? Or, I had better say, I tried to do them. I had actually managed to follow the instructions and do some exercises until I reached a fairly advanced state of relaxation or unconsciousness. Hard to say when you pass out. Lol! Well that was a hell of an exercise I must say, because at a certain moment I couldn't feel a thing anymore. My whole body was gone, vanished. So I stopped after recovering my consciousness and body of course.

Interested in some yoga classes? I could help.

....

The platform was deserted. "So strange" she thought and looked, first surprised then worried, around. "Where have they all gone?" *Although it was around rush hours there was nobody on the streets.* "The roads are empty. What happened that made it all deserted?"

She started thinking about the big city around Christmas when the streets were roaming with people. It was an evening around the holiday. A young man wearing just a T-shirt passed them by quickly and wished them or just her - she did not understand very well, a merry f...* Xmas. She was left speechless and neither did she get to answer or react in any way. Maybe it wasn't even important.

Shortly after she arrived home the news on the radio was announcing a package found near the central railway station. It contained paper, just paper, police spokesman said. White, empty paper. On the last sheet some lines were written on it, as if in a hurry.

It was a poem.

....

I wonder if thoughts can interfere with each other

....

April 28. Still

…and something else - do you remember those "net of relationships"-things that are supposed to exist everywhere, seen-unseen, at a social subatomic level?

Some say that space is in fact pretty much nothing. They mean there is so much space with nothing in it that the surrounding world would actually be built out of more or less nothing. I realize my explanation is poor but I believe you have an image of what I'm trying to say. And if it is so, how is it possible for a net of relationships to exist if the space is built of nothing? Where would this net be if the surrounding world is built of empty spaces?

This is what happens when you have nothing to do. Look at me! I'm thinking about the immortality of the soul, of the psyche. Or of the self. How many of them are there? In fact all these are nothing else but what I Am. Or what You Are.

And I, or you, filling all these empty spaces
Sleep well

On your empty space

Me

....

April 28. @:

Speaking of technique

The rows of lined up cars waiting for the green light seemed endless. "Damn it, right in the middle of the traffic! I can't hear a thing" *she said and pressed the cell phone harder to her ear.* "If I just could just have a moment of silence. I can't afford to miss this call" *she thought and closed her eyes. Everything disappeared; houses, streets, cars. Then silence. Complete silence. She opened her eyes. Nothing and no one was moving, as frozen in space and time. The image was so strange that she couldn't prevent a smile.* "Now THAT was something! So cool!" *she said to herself and felt like jumping and dancing right there, in the middle of the street.*

Did I tell you it snowed yesterday?

....

April 29, @: midnight

I don't know why I wrote to you again. Every day I promise myself I won't write and here I am again. Maybe I shouldn't have listened to that music. That jazz.

And as if it were not enough, I must be very attentive to what I'm reading. To think about what I'm thinking, about what happens around. About what others are thinking and saying, about what I used to think. About what I should be thinking and the result of the interaction between all of these together.

About the net of relationships that is around us, about E-prime (what the h*** is E-prime in fact?), about TV, wind, Guru, weather. Mathematician. Soul.

!@#$%^&*(=)-_+`~?><., :-/ !

Okay, you know that's
Me

....

She had finally understood the cause of so many arguments and why relationships were how they were.
She had walked through the city as if it was for the first time. Perhaps she didn't expect it to be so much spring.

....

Tuesday, May 13, at 4:11 AM

Yesterday I met an old acquaintance. We chit-chatted as people do when meeting each other after a fairly long time; the proper courtesy talk you know. She told me she was alone and had no reason to complain. Suddenly she made a remark about my breasts, about how huge they were. Just like that, as nothing. Breaking news! Just kidding. Truth is, compared to mine, her breasts seemed very small. But still.

Have I mentioned the nature program about exclusive species on TV last week? From a Zoo. What a price to pay for being special! How sad. In fact if you think about it we are all special creatures living in our cages. The degree of freedom is something that for us, humans, measures in money. Depending on how much money you own you can chose the "cage" to spend your life in; bigger or smaller, in lux or poverty. It's still a cage. But there is something you can never lock up and no one can take it away from you; your inner freedom.
Freedom to think.
It is something only you can build, regardless of any constraints.

Do you like theatre? I like reading theatre and visualizing the scenes, the action. Everything.
All these things…
I guess all started with an email when I pushed wrong button and sent it. So it is my fault. What a mess! How could I have mixed things up like this?

· ·

Fri., May 14, at 7:32 AM

"Who were you before you were you?"

"Even though we all identify with a very limited slice of time and space, equating "me" with one body and one mind, in reality you also live outside yourself in the field of awareness." (Adapted from "How To Know God", by Deepak Chopra, Harmony Books, 2000).(Chopra, How To Know God, 2000)

Do you remember that email about seeds to plant?

....

Saturday, May 15

Yesterday I went to the corner shop to pick up a recipe. The address sounded familiar so I paid no further attention to small text far down on the paper. Big mistake!

"Stop thinking about him! He's only doing you harm" *she heard and started to look a,round more pissed off than worried. She had woken up early in the morning to get to the airport in time and had finally managed to fall asleep despite the uncomfortable position. The guy next to her browsed indifferently through the airline magazine and those on the front and back seats were sleeping so they were unable to think consciously.* "Maybe it was right, but why would he hurt me?" *she wondered and started to feel worried about being so high in the air. Too high. There was nowhere else to run.*

"It's quite pleasant and reassuring to sit with tired people. Their mood seems to be contagious. It is so relaxing and comforting" *she said to herself. The guy woke up. She opened her eyes just as suddenly realizing she had actually been sleeping as much as he.*

Then the pressure on her lips, as if someone was trying to kiss her, woke her up.
"Maybe I'm just imagining" *she thought but the feeling was so real that she had no doubt that it hadn't been just her imagination but the reality.*
A reality

She had been reminded about the departure date several times but she hadn't really reacted. Then she realized that that day was actually the day when both of them were going to travel. He and She but to different destinations. Could they possible meet? Perhaps they will pass each other by, without even knowing it. A shade of hope crept inside her soul, somewhere.
"What if..."

I try to go outside as often as possible and not think about the existing state of facts. It's just too tragic. The journey is one of the most difficult. One morning I found, while walking, a small garden full of flowers. So beautiful! It's strange how little we need sometimes to be happy.

The city is amazing in spring. Yesterday it rained.

....

Sun., May 16, at 7:54 AM

To my friend

"As you begin to heed spirit, you can only increase in love – passion for life will appear naturally. We are like empty vessels being endlessly refilled with spirit. To be in love with someone is to share this inexhaustible flow." (Adapted by Deepak Chopra)

"Take care of Him, he's pure gold!" *she had clearly heard the morning when she was alone in her room, waiting for the taxi to take her to the station. How could she take care of him when in fact she had never had him? Perhaps her soul could take care of him.*

To try and explain the origin of thoughts would have been too much. It would have been much easier explaining the origin of dreams.

"But dreams are also thoughts we made during the non-awake state. Nightmares as well. How could I know what I dreamt of? Is it possible to control dreams?"

Sometimes she didn't know if nightmares were in fact nightmares or just regular dreams. Maybe some belong to her but what if some of the dreams belonged to others?

Sometimes I miss him madly out of nowhere, and I can't control my thoughts. They ambush me and leave me hopeless.The street I had stepped on was narrow. I stopped. We were in the middle of that empty street. Just Him and Me. Alone. We were one being.

"Think!"

"Think of what? Memories? What memories? I have to remember. But what?

When I opened my eyes I was facing a door. Above it, a wooden plaque hanging on an iron shelf was pointing towards the house on the opposite side of the street. I could hardly breathe. I read the text: "MEMOIRS". The window with bars shaped like a spider's web was staring at me.
"Net of relationships!"
Should I go back to that net of relationships which doesn't actually happen anywhere, as there is about nothing in the space between us, and all that Nothing filling this empty space would be only ME?! Or YOU?!
"Is this what I should remember? Where did I go wrong? But if it were like this, then where would HE be if he were with me? Or what would He be? Would He be I? Or my conscience? What would happen then?
I would be HIM and he would be… ME? That makes Two of ME! As in a parallel world
I think I mixed it up really well. Or did I fix it? It's one or the other.
But what if there are many more explanations?
Tomorrow I'll start the journey. I hope even this time I'll have a guardian angel with me. I HOPE

Me

....

True, May 28, at 2:24 PM

"Live in the present for it is the only moment you have" someone said.

She hadn't had fever anymore so she was able to walk around easily.
She had to walk, to mobilize. That's what her friend had been told. She leaned her back against the wall and looked at the fragile body, at the way she walked along the hall with small, fast steps. "Stop walking so fast for God sake! Save some energy. These days we all have to save some energy" she had told her friend, trying to make a joke.
She was trying to understand the person's situation even though it was difficult. There were too many things to think of. Her problems were of a different kind.

She had never known where to begin.

....

Sun., May 30, at 10:28 PM

Subject: about quantum mind

"The quantum mind or quantum consciousness hypothesis proposes that classical mechanics cannot explain consciousness, while quantum mechanical phenomena, such as quantum entanglement and superposition, may play an important part in the brain's function, and could form the basis of an explanation of consciousness." (http://en.wikipedia.org/wiki/Quantum_mind)

It was dark when she stopped. She realized she had been going for hours and had no idea where she was. She laid the purse on the sidewalk close to her and tried not to think. The gate of the house in front of which she sat, opened. "Like the gates of my soul" she thought and for a moment she remembered the day at the exhibition where all the paintings were blue. She kept waiting on the sidewalk without caring about the ones passing by. Someone, a man or maybe a young man, approached her and asked something. If she was feeling okay. She had answered without even knowing what. She had already started to cry.

She thought about her friend, about the whole situation. Did she want to forget what had happened, what she had seen? Did she have a choice? Perhaps she should have read on, discover, find out. It could have been her instead.

She was crying out loud. Alone on one edge of the sidewalk, on a random street. In a city she had just seen for the first time without knowing where she was. Without knowing anyone.

She cried a river like that time, a few days before, when she had found the email. Then she cried her heart out without being able to stop. She cried on the inside, in her mind. Intensive, quietly, without making any noise.

And she held her head for fear it would explode. And then she uttered with all of her heart, thinking of Him

Forgive me!

Simsalabim!

Tue., June 8, at: 11:24 AM

I took the book, opened it at page 57 and read: "Maxwell's equations and the secret of light."

Based on Faraday's idea according to which magnetic fields can turn into electric fields and vice versa, Maxwell wondered "what happens if they (the fields – my note) keep turning into one another, in an endless stereotype?" Researches also led him, among others, to the conclusion that "light is an electromagnetic disturbance".

Thus, "the whole electromagnetic spectrum – is nothing else but Maxwell waves", Maxwell waves which have the property to turn into one another...

Just in case

Me

....

June 10, at 4:50 AM

What would it be like if you made a wish and it came true, or if you thought of something and the next moment the person next to you, said what you only expressed in thought seconds before?

"The electromagnetic field generated by the brain is the actual carrier of conscious experience". It's what you can find on Wiki if you read about Electromagnetic theories of consciousness. Lectures like this make life worth living, don't you think so?

Have you known the first scientific studies on telepathy and paranormal phenomena were made in London in 1882, and that society still exists? The group is divided into "spiritualists" who firmly believe in the paranormal and scientists, who are more skeptical.

What they discovered scanning the brain was the way it behaves when we think. It is a kind of transmitter with which thoughts can be sent out in the form of electric impulses and electromagnetic waves of low intensity. It seems they tried to read minds with these waves, but didn't succeed.

"Some believe that telepathy is probably mediated by a fifth force, named the "psi" force, which leaves open the thought hypothesis between telepathy and quantum theory" it said in "Brain scanning", in PoI (read Physic of Impossible) at page 14. It was also said that images, thoughts, and emotions could be induced only by producing electromagnetic signals in some parts of the brain which control certain functions such as the amygdale which is responsible for producing emotions, so

....

June, at 10:25

Subject; about seeing

"Seeing is active. You send out energy, and take in energy from others. Your awareness speaks to theirs, and that is enough to create changes in the brain, leading to changes elsewhere in the body" (Adapted from Reinventing the Body, Resurrecting the Soul, by Deepak Chopra, Harmony Books, 2009)

Is this the Spiritual or the Scientist speaking now?

"Show us what you do, how you do it" someone said, or thought. The plane had already started initiating landing procedures.
"I can't, it's private", she answered trying to be polite.
The presence she felt was much too strong to be ignored. She chased the thought away and continued to look outside the plane's window. The Sun had started to go down. She could see the silver sparkles of a meandering river.

"So far, and still so close. Down there, I wonder how it will be"

And then you came along. When I had finally decided to change my life and think about myself. I had made plans. You appeared and changed everything. It was meant to be like this or maybe it was just a coincidence. Who knows?

After all that happened now I doubt there is something so divine and pure as the soul of a person that has fallen in love. No one knows how much of it is imaginary and not just physics, chemistry, biology. It's maybe some people's fantasy about a moment of immortality. Or maybe the imagination of those who naively place them on ephemeral pedestals made of wax melting at the slightest solar rain.

What is love in fact?

The truth? Science with some naivety. Nothing more. In fact science too is a form of faith but with proof or attempts to prove, a form which wants to persuade.

You know, I actually liked the texts about spirituality. They were nice, dreamy. I think I'm a dreamer and a romantic, so I believe they fit me. I wished I believed in those beautiful stories about the soul, about love. About the life we pass through without even knowing it. All we know is that, at some point, we come to a crossroads and we don't know which way to go. And we ask ourselves "Why" and "Where". Where does it lead to? A brand new life or maybe just what was meant to be, SHIVA, Eve, the BEginning of the World, Creation. The eternal questions and still the answer is unknown. Should we ever stop questioning then we'd stop existing and everything would be silence and only left would be Infinity. Space Time Soul

I am perhaps a romantic. A dreamer. Well
I am
I believe
A

Wanderer

THE JOURNEY

Notebook 1

"Though we may not understand it, the essential truth of the universe is that it's synchronistic and coincidental. Everything is connected with everything else, and if we are in synch with the universe, then we experience synchronicity." (Adapted from Power, Freedom, and Grace by Deepak Chopra, Amber- Allen Publishing Inc., 2006)

"What is the present?" I asked myself. And the answer came simply, clearly, with no effort:
"The future seen through the past"

She lay on the bed. Everything was so unfair, so hopeless. It was a race against time where you know the end will come eventually but you, in fact nobody, can't foresee it. And you have to do it. The race. Once you started it. No matter if you want to or not. And nobody asks if you are ready or not. Everybody finishes it, some earlier others later, and contrary to what we used to know and appreciate, winners always come last. The later, the better. The more you run, the less become your chances to get first to your end destination. Strange, isn't it?

"What a crowd! What on earth is going on?

What are they looking at, gathering up so close to each other on such a hot day? I must see."

When her reflection in the shop window showed up she could hardly believe that the years had changed her so much. The time spent away had taken its turn on her. She tried to find a place where she could watch what was happening

"Maybe if I asked…" she thought

Who knows, maybe they would tell me

Little things, enchants sweet words for cloudy days

At gates of dark clay, embroidered glittery

In clouds of blue wax, glowing

Turn-up till the elbow, and tight-belted

With powers only known by basil flowers,

Field flowers and perfumed fragrances

Gathered together in sparkling eyes

Full of longing

Of whispers

If you put flowers under your pillow on a summer
night, in your dream you'll see your lover to be.

June, sunny day, at: 3:24

It had been an impulse when she entered the bookshop. She looked swiftly at the shelves full of books trying to find something that could keep her busy, away from the reality outside. On an old chest of drawers, hidden by a tray and a pile of toys, lay the book. A few months before she had sent him an exemplar of it.

A piece of paper was sticking out through the pages.
"Is it possible that…" and she never finished her thought.

That night she started crying. Slowly like a whisper, then harder and harder. Without wanting to, she heard the dialogue between the two, before the door closed:
"Don't worry! I'll help you"
It was just a whisper yet clear, enough to startle her and wake her up. Not for a moment did she doubt it had been him. She closed her eyes. Tears started falling down again
Slowly In silence

⋯⋯

Thinking of a few topics, no, in fact it's only one topic – is it? – The GreatG (the great G…hm… great Gatsby? Don't think so, Google… the great? Njaaa…nope), from gravity of course, or grey matter or strings (uops, no G in the beginning! ☺. Well maybe there was no G in the beginning or, was it?), yes, I know; beating the bushes again……okay, okay… focus!

…and taking in account what those smarty pants said that the "precognition is excluded from Newtonian Physics" and that "in quantum theory, new dual states of matter are possible, such as antimatter, which is related to a matter "associated" with time passing in reverse" (I like this one), the "physicists believe that their true purpose (of the tachyons) was to provoke the Big Bang, and that is the reason why they can no longer be seen now" (Kaku, M., Physics of the Impossible, 446)(Kaku, Physics of the Impossible, 2008), it's impossible not to wonder if there are any laws, or rules and necessary and sufficient conditions for precognition to occur? Plank's constant?

I believe that when the system (space-time) detects situations of instability, it tries to re-establish symmetry by sending "advanced beams" (antimatter?).

Maybe matter works as radar. It constantly sends "beams" (maybe it's that stuff that resonates when the strings activate). When instability occurs, this is immediately detected therefore the emitted fascicules return to the source and thus travel in time.

ET voila! That is how precognition happens. Easy peasy!

In my opinion, of course☺

It had been terribly hot for several days, almost unbearable. Although the sun had set long before, the pavement of the yard was still warm. The frail breeze brought no hope that the weather would soon be milder. The two dogs, which usually sat on the stairs of the house, had been hiding in a shadowy corner. The cat had long before gone to one of the cooler rooms where the stores had been let down in time to protect against the heat.

She sat in the garden under the nut tree. Something was wrong. Almost everyone she had met was sick or about to get sick. A friend she had spoken to not long before, mysteriously disappeared. Then that colleague she had been trying to contact for a while, she finally managed to talk to, and find out his home had been robbed and the only left was the note on the empty floor about a package. Coincidences? Or maybe just bad luck?

"Maybe it will finally rain this time"

....

"This is your fault" *she was told*. "Everything happens because of you"

Is that so? So it is my fault. Eventually

....

June, at: 3:00 PM

Subject: seekers are never lost

"Spirit often begins to speak: narrow escapes, lucky accidents and intuitions that come true. The real question isn't "Why did this happen?" but "Why did this happen to me?" (Adapted after Deepak Chopra)
But how does this happen, is a far more interesting question.

The postman had personally handed him the package that day. It was a book she had sent him on his birthday. Only five minutes after he had entered the house, the phone rang.

"Happy birthday!" she said.

"Oh hi, thank you! How did you know…", *he said visibly surprised by the coincidence.*

She leafed through the TV guide trying to find something interesting. She almost fell asleep when strange, sunken sounds outside made her switch her thoughts and startle. Then, the doorbell. She was completely awake.

"Who could be so late?" *she said almost loud more to encourage herself. The neighbors were visiting friends on the countryside so she was the only one left in the house. It was past midnight when the doorbell rang again. She waited a moment without moving, without breathing. She tossed her head on the pillow. Now the voices seemed angry, threatening and much more distinct.*

"Where is that stupid telephone?" *she wondered and looked around terrified. She always left it somewhere and then she had to turn the house upside down to find it.*

"I should have had it with me right now. Why can't you find things when you really need them?"

She turned off the lights and pulled the blanket over her head like she used to do when she was a little girl and she was home alone trembling at any sound on the old floor.

She tried to think of something else. Then there was complete silence as if nothing had happened.

"Where could they have vanished? And how did it happen so fast? I should have heard their steps on stairs"

She didn't know anyone who would pay a visit so late in the night. She closed her eyes but she could not fall asleep for several hours.

"Maybe it was a mistake after all. Someone must have knocked at the wrong door"

Could we really influence the course of events? I hoped that things would change if I saw them rather positively.

I hoped he had had a good day as well.

The day when she called him driven by impulse, she was rather surprised to see she had called him shortly after he had entered. Startled by the uniqueness of the moment, she did not know what to say. Just waited, wanting to hear him, to know it was not just an image, a thought.

That he truly existed.

....

Still June

It was one of the few times when she allowed herself a break. She drank her coffee silently.

The young couple on the pavement across the street walked without a hurry. The sun was almost at dusk and the breeze filled the atmosphere with the rich perfume of the lilacs. A teenager was talking on the phone unveiling fragments of the conversation. Not much later on, a young man came to keep her company. Their talk, at first rather sonant, gradually transformed into whispers. She imagined how those two were him and her, walking the same road, sitting at the same table.

Forging dreams. Time and space. Life.

This song is familiar. I had always enjoyed listening to it but not this time.

Unwillingly I thought again of the numerous situations which had occurred, of events which many times seemed rather weird and inexplicable.

Now I knew, or at least I thought I knew, what had happened and why.

What is the soul?

....

She had not cried for years. If it had ever happened those around her would have considered such a natural thing out of norm..

That day, when terrified she realized she could have been the person lying almost unconscious on the small bed, she started crying. She cried in the street. She cried on the train. She cried in the cab ignoring the driver who out of pity, or maybe just curiosity, asked her how she was feeling.

"I'm just a little tired", she had answered. "Just a little tired" and she tried her best not to burst into tears again.

Back in Time

June -14

À propos waves…

"As for Maxwell's equations on light, there are two possible results, a "delayed" wave, representing the standard movement of light from one place to another as well as an "advanced" wave when the fascicle of light goes back in time. This advanced result comes from the future and goes in the past." (Kaku, M., Physics of Impossible, 436)

Since talking about it, perhaps if we could control these waves, we would be able to send messages in time regarding future events. Why not?

Think. The delayed ones (waves), representing the standard movement of light, they are also traveling in time but in only one direction (young ladies don't get crazy now! No, it's not *that* One Direction! Unnecessary comment because no young person will read this. Wonder if someone else will ever read it. But let's not underestimate the young generation) – where was I?

Yes, here

…they are also traveling in time introducing a ΔDelta (you know, delta, as in math), since they are delayed. Then the "advanced" ones, supposed to travel forth and back in time, they are traveling on the same trajectory, supposing time has only one direction and is linear, and then you have 2timesΔ T (deltaT), which are different, of course, because they (the waves) never return exactly at the starting point. This could mean that they are not following exact the same path back but can take other trajectories depending on… have no idea on what, in which Case, one should introduce in the equation not only deltaT but deltaStoo. Or something like that. Something measuring the other dimension, or dimensions, of Time because if the advanced waves exist and travel in time, then the time is not linear, with only one dimension.

And that's why we are traveling in time back and forth, aside, up and down, in zigzag, chaotically too many times.

If it were this way, hypothetically speaking, we may say that everything around us is matter in an oscillatory state, including ourselves. Given the existence of antimatter in much smaller quantities than matter, as residues of a primordial explosion as the opposing characteristics of matter versus antimatter and supposing there were sources where the concentration of antimatter was excessive, irrespective of the form this source would take, then the result of the union between matter and antimatter would be various forms of anomalies, including the human one.

· ·

Then we may think what the world would look like. There may be economic and financial collapses, natural or social disasters. Or they may be alright. There may be no wars, love may become a religion and nobody would die from incurable contagious diseases. No rich, nor poor. A new human species may exist. There may only be matter and antimatter in perfect harmony. Life may be with no real frame. No beginning or end, like a "perpetum mobile" of dreams and wishes transposed on the mega screen of a virtual existence.

There may be

Me

· ·

June, 16ᵗʰ

I let fate decide this time as well. I opened the book randomly and read:

"Is precognition possible on Earth nowadays? In fact, precognition can hardly intertwine with modern physics, as it comes against the principle of cause, as well as the law of cause and effect"

Is it possible that our encounter may have been established beforehand or was it just chance that I found his address among so many others. Why did I contact him? Or maybe He contacted me. Either way it is a fact that many things have changed since.

Were it true that time-travelling fascicles of antimatter really existed, warning us about what was going to happen in time and space, in dimensions three or four, in a probable existence, then it would be possible for us to establish in which of the worlds we are going to spend our lives only by the simple focus of thoughts, letting ourselves be led by the non-local. Cool, isn't it?!

If there are any "advanced" fascicules travelling in the future, then one may explain those moments when we predict whom we are going to meet or what is going to happen. Those flashes, travelling waves, may prove facts which are to happen in a yet to be written future therefore much easier to be abandoned or transformed. Then we could change fate, we could change what was already supposed to happen. Then we could become the forgers of our own lives. Or fate. Or whatever you call it. How interesting, how fascinating would life be, given we knew the moment what it was going to happen. No surprises, no uniqueness of the spontaneous. No
One

But then how would it be possible to predict that we are going to meet someone we know?

Given the fact that everything surrounding us, including ourselves, was matter or antimatter and that everybody absorbs and emits energy simultaneously, then these advanced waves would be capable to detect certain frequencies of the persons or objects to interfere with, and which are probably codified by the subconscious (NOW we are talking about Quantum Physics!), the subconscious being the coded properties the matter has at quantum level at a given point in space and time that defines you, and anything else.
Therefore the advanced waves can scan the environment like radar, go back to the source, at quantum level, and generate reactions which stimulate the cerebral area that controls the forming of images, ideas and

feelings, thoughts, in this way enabling the visualization of what is to be encountered and pre-cognizable.

This would mean that the soul, the conscience is nothing but time traveling matter. Antimatter, information coming from future in order to re-establish a possible imbalance of the system we define and in which we act.

June 17th, @: 12, 58

Feynman discovered that "an electron that travels back in time is the same thing as an anti-electron travelling in the future" and that these "retroactive" results represented the "antimatter movement", that if "an electron hits an anti-electron, the two annihilate each other and form a gamma radiation" (Kaku, M., Physics of the Impossible, 438, 439)

Early in the morning she decided to join the others on the trip. She packed hastily a few things and before she got out, she stopped for a moment and wondered whether to take the wallet and the keys or not. She was going to come back with the others; either way they were useless in the middle of nowhere, in the woods. But at the very last moment she changed her mind and threw them in the backpack.

When she got out of the car, she realized it was hotter than she had expected. Despite the early hour, the temperature was already high, promising an unbearable hot day. She gave up walking down the road, the flowers, the landscapes, even the company. It was much too hot. Suffocating! Her breath slowed down after a short distance and every time she inhaled, the hot air seemed to burn her throat.

It had been a while before the first car to got ahead of hers. The shadow of the tall trees on both sides of the road was soothing. The heat turned everything to silence. The breezes of air were rare, almost unperceivable and nothing allowed the clouds to suddenly appear at the horizon.

It was a strange feeling being alone on the deserted road. And yet she felt safe. It was quiet. The ridge could be perceived clearly with every single detail making the distance miraculously disappear.

"How it is up there? The view must be thrilling" *she said and stopped for the third time in the past five minutes.*

Not once was she up there to admire the landscape. For a moment she wondered if it had not been a good idea to take the cabin and climb, to go to the hut, but realized that in fact she only had a little change of clothes.

Despite of the nice weather the temperature may have dropped a lot during the night at that altitude.

She managed to arrive on time in the city and take the taxi back home. Eventually taking the keys and the wallet proved to be a good idea.

The Visit

She almost could not believe her eyes how much the person had changed. Seeing each other again was short and the dialogue reminded her that too much time it might have passed since they had last seen each other.

Waves of hot steam rose from the pavement making everything look as if seen through a distorted mirror. Huge parasols covered the summer garden with a comforting shadow.

Although it was long before lunch all the tables were immediately filled and the waiters started showing up one by one, taking orders with exaggerated smiles. Suddenly she remembered the acquaintance she was going to meet shortly.

"How could I forget!?" *she said and dialed the number just to realize the battery was dead.*

"That's weird, it had not been long since I charged it and now…" *and as if it wasn't enough, her visiting friend's phone stopped also working.*

It was then, when the woman at the next table offered to help. With swift unexpected moves, the person took the phone from her hand and dialed. Everything had happened so fast that she did not have time to react. The friends were equally surprised. They looked at each other without commenting and then, all of a sudden, started to talk to get over the awkward moment. She only had time to turn her head around and see that the woman had disassembled her phone into pieces and wrote something on a piece of paper.

"Excuse me but what are you actually doing?" *she asked her and the tone of her voice was rather unpleasant.* "I wish you gave me the phone immediately", *she said and reached her hand in a way that allowed no comment or doubt about what was going to happen.*

"Nothing, I was just checking. I mean trying to help" *the woman dodged and watched above her sun glasses in a way that looked innocent while pouting her intensely red colored lips. Then hastily she put the phone back together, took the purse she had held in her arms all this time, and vanished.*

They were taken aback. They looked at each other without saying a word obviously shocked by what had happened. What had it all been about? The next moment a cold shiver went down her spine and made her feet weak. She realized her phone contained all the necessary information to access the bank accounts of the contacts she had.

....

An Idea

Sitting here at home, in the yard or in the garden, thinking about my (SF!) conclusions about soul, about matter travelling in time (by the way, this thing I discovered while I was shaving my legs), I had a flashback, an idea, an image.In fact everything that happened on the trip was so ordinary, so usual and yet it all had a hidden, unlikely meaning regarding matter and antimatter. And soul. Everything was so simple.

If the soul is matter that travels back in time (read antimatter), it may be that, when I was preparing to go on the trip, these advanced waves had already arrived in the future, "saw" what had happened and came back in time to "tell" me to take my keys and wallet. So what happened during the trip, in the future, would have happened before I had left home, before I had stepped out the door. Between the thought if I should take the wallet and the keys, and the almost simultaneous thought that was the decision to take them.

And *That* was precognition!

Or whatever you want to call it.

Or what the Devil makes when it weighs its tail&!

Sometime in June

Today I was sitting at the table being philosophical:

If antimatter is matter travelling in time, and we apply this very judgment to the grammar pronunciation by linking the grammar terms with the physics, this would mean that "to be" is the equivalent of matter, and "not to be" of antimatter. Together they annihilate themselves similar to when an electron collides with an anti-electron resulting in gamma radiations.

Okay! But this would explain why in certain cases "to be" becomes "not to be". Maybe this is the case when things are inexplicably done the other way round by those which are charged with antimatter. And absorb antimatter. And that is E-PRIME. Bingo!

Thank you! Thank you! I'm flattered. Now, let me proceed.

Where was I? Yes, and then I thought:

"To be", a lexical notion, may be an expression of the fourth dimension which is TIME, a phonetic definition of an existential process represented in time, with beginning and end.

So in these cases or forms of expression, time has got a better defined and limited dimension which means that from the point of view of the advanced wave beams, the emitted wave would reach the limit of the process (time-space) and then would come back as antimatter. That is why what "is" would be the same thing with "is not" in quantum theory.

But

If the form of expression is probabilistic, we "may" say that a time-space system is limitless and matter in form of wave beams travels freely. This would be a continuous process, possible, ∞ or a horizontal 8, that is the INFINITE, until the system found its own balance limits.

When we say "is", this means an automatic delimitation of a "space-time" system that immediately excludes the existence of unpredictable processes that would change the trajectory of the fascicle of waves emitted by the source/object, waves that "scan" the future. This would mean that a time-space system was or is a perfect system, which is very unlikely.

I wonder what Shakespeare thought when he came up with "to be or not to be". Was it The Maxwell laws? Dirac, Feynman? Was it the delayed, or the advanced waves?

Maybe matter. Antimatter?

....

Somewhere, still June, @ 9:05?

In the narrow stock-yard, there was a rooster and some hens. Next to them, separated by a fence, three little pigs lay in a thin layer of dust and dried mud.

"Can animals feel happiness? Maybe if they were free" *she thought and the next moment one of the birds, a little grey ordinary one, got out of the pen and vanished behind the house.* "It looks like sometimes you have to seek and fight until you find your way to freedom" *she said thinking for a moment of her very own being. She realized that in fact it could have been possible to meet him, that the gate had opened letting inside thoughts and actions, possibilities and wishes.*

Would she be happy to see him?

After so many years she had finally managed to find the "crack" in her space, or time, leaving open a new unknown road. A road with so many words left unspoken and so many mysteries to decipher.

For so many years she felt herself imprisoned, caught in a modern cage, like some sort of interesting experiment. Left with only her thoughts and feelings.

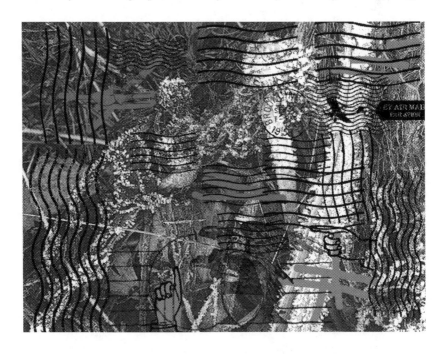

A one-player game, with unwritten rules known by no one
A game of souls and thoughts, and grammar times
Or maybe just mega, or micro, dimensional time
Matter. Antimatter – "advanced" waves
A form of existence which begins in infinite, and a finite with no end
With immeasurable plasticity and the unpredictable toughness
Of wandering stars

．．

She left one morning unexpectedly without saying a word. She only packed her bags and managed to catch the last train. Had she been selfish? Maybe. But it had been too much and actually no one knew how it had been for her.

And it seemed no one cared for her, for how she felt. Nothing else mattered now. Soon she was going to leave.

...and only now did I realize that parallel worlds actually exist, and that each and every one of us actually lived them every single day without thinking about or understanding the phenomenon. I realized that another multidimensional world could exist and it would be as real as the one we use to call real.

I realized that our relationship had not changed.

At all

．．

June, at: 7:29

The car's window was fully opened letting her breath in the warm air.

She failed to do anything but watch life passing by so fast, so impersonally. So irreversibly, undoubtedly and before time, knowing it. It was totally inappropriate to tell everything the way she had told him. They had not seen each other for years and still she trusted him and opened her heart out. Had she reached that moment in future when is possible to travel back in time and become younger, living in parallel universes?

If matter and antimatter accumulated in our bodies should unify, then we would become one single electron. Might be true. And then? Then governed by those laws of, let's call it, love, we can decipher the mystery of life and universe or whatever governs everything around us. Nice. It remains only a tiny problem. What is the mathematical, but I suspect there is some itsy-bitsy chemistry stuff involved here as well, formula of L O V E?

Someone? Anyone?!

The Hut

The tom cat cuddled his head onto her neck, snuggling her. She stood like that, laying in the shadow of the old tree, caressing him. He started purring.

The guest house was hidden by a fence of ornamental trees. The room, painted in a bright yellow, reminded her of the summer day when, driven by impulse, she asked him to take her to the beach.

"Lovely! Two lovers spending a few days outside the big city in the middle of nowhere, away from civilization and its facilities" she murmured for herself watching the young couple arriving.

"Nice car too. They seem to afford quite a few things these guys" she said and followed with a jealous eye the sport car stopping silently outside the entrance.

It could have been the way they acted and talked, or maybe the way the landlord himself received them that made her pay them more attention.

"Better to keep them away. You never know who people are nowadays" she thought then suddenly she got the feeling she had seen the couple before. Doesn't matter how hard she tried she couldn't place them.

....

That evening, years ago, she went for a walk in the empty low lit streets. There was a place she knew before where she could watch the stars undisturbed. At the horizon the lightning piercing through the skies made everything look dramatic. Somewhere there was a storm.

It was The Light in the middle of the sacred night, an orgasm of streams and music from the sky, from the starry abyss of above.

....

Although it was not what she wanted, she managed to make them believe she was interested in their dialogue. Now they were walking together on the narrow twined path trying to make time pass. They had insisted to go up to the crest and she knew that it was a very bad idea. Given the weather they would not have gone too far.

They had climbed some hundreds of meters when the rain started. The sky seemed to have become lower, wrapping the crest and the valley to the horizon. She descended to a hidden fir tree making her a bed of savin and grass, took the notebook and started writing.

The couple gave up climbing the crest.

"No really mountain lovers" she said watching the two sitting near a fir tree.

"It looks like these guys just run around without knowing where to take the road. They seem pretty much lost unless…"

Dinner was a quiet affair in the empty dining hall. It had been a long day with bad weather that forced them to change their plans.

The door opened noisily making the glasses on the table vibrate. The gust of wind that filled suddenly filled the whole room brought rain with it all the way to their table. In the poorly-lit dining room they almost didn't notice the stranger that showed up in the doorway. He was covered in a huge rain cloak with the hat pulled down to the base of the nose. He sat down at the nearest table and placed his gnarled hands in the sign of a prayer. He sat that way for a long time without saying a word, without making a gesture. The waiter appeared unexpectedly behind him with the suddenness of a ghost, to disappear just as unexpectedly and inexplicably as he had arrived.

She knew she shouldn't do it but now she was starting to worry that the two lovers hadn't managed to leave earlier. The road back down to the village was horrible in this kind of weather and anything was possible. The truth was that she had wished for rain. She'd seen it in her mind. And it came in strong gusts, with thunder and lightning flashing across the landscape over large distances.

Nothing special

The coffee, still steaming, spread rich flavor all over the room. It was the best moment of the day when she could gather her thoughts while enjoying the hot drink. From her window she could see how the first rays of the sun turned the ridge in purple. The storm had lasted almost till dawn but there was no trace of the night before.

The voices were low and stressed. Tiptoeing, she got closer to the door:

"I must leave. I am screwed if I miss the connection again", the voice said full of fear.

"I have to get rid of the package"

"Okay, we can do this together and..." but the whispers this time were so low that the rest of the conversation disappeared. An opened door, quick feet on the stairs then a muffled sound like something or someone had fallen and rolled, made her startle.

"As far as I know, the rooms upstairs are still under construction. They should have been unoccupied" she thought and her eyes frantically searched the room for a way to escape.

She felt her body slide along the door on the floor.

The village was like any other village of its kind. Nothing special. The main street, on either side of which identical houses were spread out, went from one side of the village to the other in a perfect straight line as if measuring the shortest way between the beginning and the end of an unknown circle of life.

At the kiosk, the only one and the main attraction in the whole village, a fairly round middle aged man had spread the few products, food and chemicals, gardening tools and plastic toys, all together on the few existing shelves. It was early in the morning but already hot and sticky. And it would only get more so. The old rusty fan placed on the shelf between an apple and a perfume bottle worked hard to cool down the little man's sweaty body. A few children were playing in the middle of the empty road. Throwing water at each other from old plastic bottles proved to be a cool idea after all.

Glued on the thin wall next to a pile of cobs, the ad showed the face of a seven-year-blue eyed girl. Her innocent crooked smile revealed two missing front teeth. She stopped and read. The girl had inexplicably gone missing a few days ago from her front yard, puzzlingly as none of the other children or adults could say what had happened to her.

A substantial sum had been offered for any information.

The telephone number one could call was written in large, red numbers.

She hurried to the guest house. The idyllic image of the village with picturesque landscapes had suddenly changed and been replaced by foreboding.

Laid down in the grass she looked at the sky. Not a cloud. Without her having seen or heard them, the sheep dogs had surrounded her, smelt her and went back to their herd as if she were merely a completely uninteresting obstacle. Strange that she hadn't been afraid. In fact she had been calm, tranquil. Safe in their midst. She had felt free.

"It really is beautiful here. And quiet."

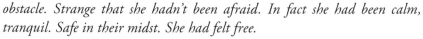

It was her first night alone, away from everyone and everything. It was the middle of the night and she couldn't tell if she had been dreaming or not. The headache made her feel as if her head was about to explode. When she opened her eyes her gaze fell on the plasma TV, an unusually large screen for such a small room.

"Plasma is the fourth state of matter – liquid, solid, gas and plasma. Ionized atoms" *she vaguely remembered having read that somewhere.*

"Thunder and lightning are nothing more than matter in plasma form, right?"

The crisscrossing and horizontal lines repeated themselves in an intermittent flow with the same characteristic annoying noise. Then someone had made her work out. She was tired and wanted to quit, to stop. Her eyes were heavy, impossible to open when she felt how someone was pinching her hips. She tried to say something but couldn't open her mouth. She never understood how everything happened but when the counting came to ten and the person stopped, she opened her eyes. She was alone and the room was the same. The bed was the same. Everything was the same. Except she.

She was definitely not the same.

"Who can that be?" she wondered and watched puzzled how the man that had parked the car in front of her window opened the trunk, revealing two enormous leather bags.

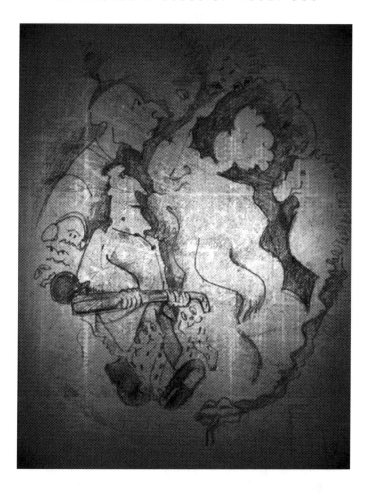

His eyes were unusually small. The nose rose triumphal as a slightly emaciated pyramid on the almost squared pale surface of his face. The flashy green clothes with big oil stains looked more like a uniform, loosely picked from the pile with unwashed clothes rather than regular mountain-holiday ones.

"Why would he need those bags in the mountains?" she said and continued to watch hidden behind the pale orange drape.

"His face seems familiar but where to put him? I am sure I have seen him before"

Suddenly the image of the village came like a flash and made her startle.

"The guest house!" she whispered. She had seen him skulk around the same night the couple arrived.

"He never dared to enter the courtyard" she said, "the day before I arrived at the hut in the mountain."

It was almost dinner time when the blonde, showed up next to him as he was unpacking. She'd been abrupt with him, telling him he was no longer needed. She insisted that he should not wait for her and had to repeat it a few times on a rising note of scorn, mockingly. The man had suddenly grabbed her arm and tried to push her into his car. The front door of the bungalow opened and a young man showed up.

She was still behind the curtain unable to react or say a thing. She had felt a void in her stomach and a sensation that had turned her legs to rubber. She had never had that feeling before but she knew she was about to faint when the door to the room opened and the two lovers from the guest house showed up:

"Shall we? We have to eat before we leave. The weather will get worse. It's about to start raining."

They left the room after a complete silent dinner. The moment they had reached the hallway, the uniform man appeared unexpectedly behind her. He was just a few steps away, so close she could feel his breath. Shivers of dread made her startle. She walked faster to catch up with the couple.

A strong gust of wind came from the forest when a raindrop splashed on her cheek.

"Will they make it in time?"

5:45 am

"A cup of coffee would be great now" she thought and stretched to reach the phone hidden somewhere under the pile of papers and books. She turned it on.

"Almost six"

She skimmed through the received messages without paying them much attention.

"Nothing, nothing, and nothing. I should delete them all. Unless" and stopped. Her heart began to beat at faster, irregular throbs.

"The package" she'd managed to read the text and felt breathless.

"Those two young persons, the blonde and her guy, had talked about a package. They had to deliver a package somewhere in a city".

The sign automatically moved to the next message.

"General. General? Who the heck is the General? General as in general, or...a General. Who had sent these messages? Someone must be joking with me. The phone number is unlisted"

The sound of steps outside her door became clearer. Someone knocked on the door:

"At six o'clock in the morning?!"

No One's Land

I had started to rub my hands together to warm them. It was the middle of summer but a pair of gloves would have been good now. The sun had not risen yet. The morning chill permeated the clothes moistened in the nearly knee-high grass. The only road led to the hut and to the nearby seismological station. I knew it since I had spoken to the shepherd that sheltered his flock nearby, where the road curved.

"This is not a good idea. I might provoke the dogs."

But I went on my way. I was close to the sheepfold gate when I heard the dogs starting to bark.

"Perhaps if I ignore them they would let me be."

I kept on when the grass rustled behind me. I half turned and looked over my shoulder. Two hounds had sprung out of nowhere. Two four-legged moving shadows.

They were no longer barking. They were making a menacing, rolling sound, deep in their throats, revealing their sharp fangs. Their eyes were staring at me. I continued walking. They were now four. They didn't seem as friendly as they were when they had stood in the grass hidden among the sheep, when they had surrounded and ignored me. Had I stepped on their turf? I don't think so.

Perhaps it was the smell or that sense of responsibility, the fear of their owner. Perhaps this is what they had been taught to do, to obey the orders. If they failed to do so, they would be given no food or water. They would be harshly punished.

The day before, when I had spoken to the shepherd, one of hounds had come to me. It had lifted its head and looked at me as if to say:

"Take care of me, pet me please. It's been a long time since anyone has taken care of me."

She lifted her paw, put his head in my lap and gently closed its eyes. I petted it.

I stopped. I felt how my heart had started running without control.

"I must remain calm" and I waited.

I listened to their barking. Were they warning me, or was it just a way of communicating with me, sending me a message? I tried to ignore them or to understand. Who I was, who I am. What I was doing there on their turf alone and without an owner or companion, not being afraid of them. Just curiosity

My sheer curiosity

A familiar feeling of hate and defiance, of contempt, pity and revulsion took hold of her.

She was back in time, long ago, when she had tried to discover the secret of the place. She had been unlucky enough to be there, for a short time but enough to realize that things were not as they should be - that something utterly strange and illegal was going on behind closed doors. Perhaps she shouldn't have been so curious, she shouldn't have asked questions and investigate. Drawing conclusions. She should have turned a blind eye. Huge sums of money seemed to have been involved in. How many of them knew what all that was about?

She remembered what had happened then, during all those years. She was in an artificial world, a windowless world without the possibility of breathing. It was a world in which she had moved without having been able to see.

....

I looked to the ridge, then away to the valley lost in the fog. I was besieged by them and they had stopped barking. I ignored them or tried to do that. I don't know why I felt sure of myself, confident, afraid of nothing and no one. I felt safe, stronger than ever. I was in their midst but at the same time far away. Unreachable, untouchable. I was inaccessible as if surrounded by a protective wall. It had happened before when everything closed from the outside, or from the inside, leaving nothing outside or within.

It was that peculiar sensation when a feeling of hate or love, or terrible fury, had caused what was about to happen in the next moments. It was a sort of serenity, of boundless peace of mind where nothing and no one could reach the deepest, most hidden secrets of the soul. It was as it had happened other times before when isolated by the void outside, disconnected but still tied to the world, I could be anywhere, and nowhere.

Here or there

In multiple universes

I was matter or anti-matter. I was that state I have lived over and over a number of times.

I was the thought. Spirit. I was soul.

Nothing else mattered.

It was then when I clearly saw shadows of the past and dreams of the future were woven in a fascinating tapestry of thin, graceful threads of ephemeral times. I was matter in different stages of decomposition, trying to compress time and space in spheres of exuberant shapes.

Phantasmagorical sparkling shards of colored glass kept in gilded cauldrons, in shining cow dung in the shape of a fortress.

I was there quietly watching them, seemingly uncaring. In a different time

In a different space

In a dimension of quantum, and destiny

Of serenity

Of coordinates X, Y, Z or T

I was in No One's Land

....

If only I could control them by concentrating my thoughts.
"Best friends!" I said and waited.

I waited for the thought to arrive in electromagnetic waves, to decompose so as then rearrange itself in the drawers of their grey matter, finding the specific patterns for each wave length. When these would be properly calibrated at cellular, atomic quantum level, replicating the same model as was transmitted in the oscillating matter, then the information would have reformed in exactly the same form it had been transmitted in, namely that of thought. And the wish will have been received, decoded, displayed, translated and interpreted in what would be similar to a transcendental discussion.

I remembered how calm I had been a day before when they had surrounded me as I lay in the grass. I was calm now as well, surprisingly so. Perhaps it was only a sensation, a wish. It was a choice I had made, the only one that would have been reasonable and possible. Had I run, they would have surely attacked me. So I stayed.
"Best friend" I repeated in my head.
The next moment the biggest and more insistent hound, most likely the pack leader, turned around and disappeared soundlessly without looking back. To my amazement the other hounds followed it. I felt greatly relieved to see them go. I continued to remain still without looking away, without breathing. Minutes had passed since they had left and I was still frozen in the same place. I looked forward. Unseeing, unfeeling. I moved away with small, measured steps toward the hut. I desperately wanted a cup of coffee.

....

NOW I was awake, aware of what was happening around me. Aware too of the monstrosity of human existence, of the spiritual baseness surrounding me like a low quality movie with excessively decadent colors in a picture that is off-center, overused, with whorish breaks and disdainful commercials.
I could see thoughts, ideas.

NOW I was really awake. When I stopped by the hut everything was calm. And I only could see

The View. Birds
And Clouds
I only could feel the Breeze
The Sun
And Silence
Nothing more

Was it anything else but what I longed for? To get away from it all, and to be free. To escape fear through fear, and through fear discover peace.

To Seize the Moment. Discover it.

Middle of the night, June, was it …the 13th?

It was all about different states of matter and transformation, chemical and biological, at quantum level, matter that interacts with anomalies while interrupting the flow, and plenitude (the prelude?),of the universal law of gravity or whatever this gravity is called before we name it.

Well the Law of gravity it is called Gravity because the guy (Newton, right?) named it so. It could have been called something else like the law of… well I do not know right now what it could have been called but maybe he couldn't find something better.

The truth is I think, in my humble opinion, that we are not discovering facts; we are just giving names by sometimes understanding things around us. And then, wow, what a discovery! We are kind of playing seriously with eternity, with something that has already been gone for the un-compressive code of time and un-decoded paths of the secret Grail. Unspeakable, unread. Untouchable. Waiting for someone to get answers and restart all over again.

If light from already disappeared stars is coming to us in a, let say, parallel sort of existence, then what if we already have been a part of that existence and only shadows we are now, and the only true of us has remained in a distant future or past.

Deities

She rescued the book from the pile of clothes strewn about when she'd unpacked. For a long time she has been in the habit of carrying it with her everywhere. She kept trying to read it, thinking they would meet and talk about it.

She opened the book and began leafing. What she read was special and completely unexpected:

"Historically speaking, so important was reading minds perceived that it was often associated with deities. A true telepath, who could easily read people's thoughts, could easily slip in a banker's head or blackmail rivals. He would be a threat to the security of the governments –being able to effortlessly steal the most sensitive secrets of any nation. He would be feared and, probably, hunted!" (Kaku, M., Physics of the Impossible, 137)

"What about that telepath they are talking about that terrifies everyone around?"*she said and looked away from the book to an unspecified point on the wall.*

"…and all those scientists that are trying to find out more. But what they haven't managed to discover" *she said, this time putting one of her nasty joyful smile on her face,* "or are simply not taking into consideration when they make their calculations, is the birth of a mutant" *she almost shouted out the word like a mooing cow* "named The Mule. Hmmm, if that guy is really, really capable of controlling everyone's minds over large distances and capable of controlling everyone and everything…. Wow! That's something!"

"If I think about it, *she said looking at the ceiling,* the mule describes me perfectly!"

On the wall, next to the bathroom door, she saw the coat rack. The hook was shaped like the horn of an Aries.

"My zodiac sign, what a coincidence!"

So captivated was she by the text that she continued reading. At page 116 she read the following:

"The science historians have tried very hard to discover exactly what Schrodinger was doing when he had discovered the famous equation that would change the landscape of modern physics and chemistry."

The fact is that Schrodinger (between breake, who liked to party quite a lot – media info, btw) took Broglie's material waves – I have no idea who this one is, if he's still alive – and extracted the equations that would bear his name for the electrons.

Difficult stuff, hard to understand. At least for me.

So, the scientists wanted to know what this guy, Schrodinger, was doing when he discovered this and that. Apparently he was a believer in free love, and not only did he take his wife on holidays with him but also his mistresses. On top of that he kept a journal about his amorous liaisons, with codes for each meeting. Actually I don't know why I wrote this short parenthesis, but my thoughts lead me to consider what does love (hmm, perhaps just sex) has to do with physics. The question is if anyone has ever written a mathematical equation of love.

Okay, sex.

What happens in the body at a microscopic level when you make love, to the electrons along with all kinds of waves, with matter and anti-matter? A burst of energy and perhaps gamma radiation

Bubbles, bubbles

New universes, anti-universes. Traveling back in time, tissue regeneration

Bubbles, bubbles, bubbles

In the case of anti-matter, if the processes were reversed then youth without age and eternal life would be possible.

!

Bubbles

....

She got up abruptly.

The quick and vulgar threatening voices were so loud that it was impossible to ignore them. Then a slammed door and the tires of a car as it skidded noisily. She stopped reading and strained to hear what was happening outside. It was late and much too dark to see anything. The weather had been terrible and the road down to the village was dangerous. Carefully she shut the window and then tiptoeing pressed her ear to the door.

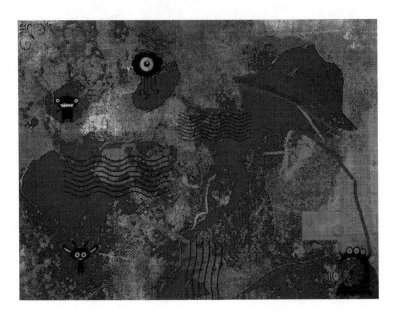

She held her breath for a moment. The noises seemed
to have been absorbed by the night.

She checked once again that the door was locked then turned on the TV.
It made her feel less alone. She opened the book again at page 146, "Scans of
the brain", and continued to read:

"Telepathy is believed to be mediated by a fifth force, called "psi", which leads the door open to the theory that connects telepathy and quantum physics."

Then further on:

"By introducing radioactive sugar in the bloodstream, the latter pools in areas of the brain that are activated by the thinking process; thereby graphically representing the pattern created by anti-matter in the living brain, which can also represent the thinking patterns."

"The gravitational, electromagnetic force "psi", photons, tachyons, the Higgs' boson…"

She had read about these forces or terms and had reached to certain
conclusion, her own. The book seemed to come from the realm of fantasy,
of science fiction. Everything was science in a language everyone could
understand. She should have been able to understand.

Was it about the inflation theory? About the monopoles or about the theory of chaos when the system has reached a certain organizational, or perhaps energetic level? When the system was re-balancing, was re-arranging in a superior form, in a new reference system with three or perhaps four dimensions. Another XYZ coordinates system.

I believe that the discussion on the XYZ coordinates system, as we have been traditionally taught in school that XYZ coordinates would represent three dimensions, XYZ is pretty interesting.

There is sometime a fourth dimension, the negative one. But as far as quantum physic is concerned with, there seems to be several more dimensions. Ten?Eleven? Maybe thirteen. How then would the coordinate system look like with ten dimensions? And how would these dimensions be measured or represented in a system of axes of coordinates?

For a long time she had though that it was just fate that had made things happen. She thought it was something that only happened to her.

She was lying on the bed and trying to muse. Would everything she had read about parallel worlds make any sense? Were they important regarding everything that had happened so far? All those coincidences and then the discussions about the soul, about conscience and about another world, a spiritual one…a world of atoms, unseen and yet all encompassing. A world with beginning and without end. With start in infinity

Was this the reason that made her to "get out", to come here in the middle of nature? She needed a clean environment, pure and unaffected. She needed to think freely, to be herself. To meditate. However hard she may have tried to understand she couldn't find a plausible mathematical explanation. It all seemed too incredible. And yet all these things had happened. It was the reason why she had started to write, to read. And then she started to see things from a different perspective, with a different type of curiosity.
More intensely
More alertly

She hadn't thought about him in a long while.
What was he doing?

Itsy Bitsy Spider

That night, after coming back from the cinema, they had made love. Interesting how his tone had suddenly changed. Maybe she was just imagining it. He had become more focused, more serious. They started talking about the movie they had seen and all of a sudden he had asked her for how long she had been speaking English, and at what age she had started learning it in school. He asked her if she was Asian, a strange and completely unexpected question. No one had asked her that before. Then she remembered that same day, in the car, he had chosen her favorite songs to listen to. Perhaps it had been a coincidence but she had been so surprised to hear exactly those songs she had listened to so often, that she had never stopped wondering how it had been possible. She tried to remember the moment in which she had told him what she liked. When they met the first time, she told him about herself, about traveling. What else had she told him?

An unpleasant feeling of insecurity and fear, of the unknown, started to creep around her shadowing those wonderful moments lived not so long ago, when they were hugging and offering themselves one another. Actually it wouldn't have been something unusual. She remembered he liked jazz. Nothing weird about that but why had he turned so serious, so strange? And his questions seemed odd, inappropriate. She didn't really know him. She tried to calm herself.

"Maybe he had been simply curious. Just a question that was asked without any other reason" she thought.

Even so, she wanted to ask him so many things. She wished she could talk to him, to tell him more about herself, about her thoughts. About her feelings

About him

Back to Future

July, the 4th

"In science fiction stories, the tachyons are usually used to send messages back in time, for clairvoyants."

"So interesting, really interesting" *she said and almost fell on the floor from the chair she was sitting on. She continued to read:*

Cool! I knew I had read somewhere about tachyons. So this stuff would have existed from the beginning and helped the universe go bang. How big, no one knows exactly.

"Feinberg believes that the emission of a forward moving tachyon that is traveling through time is identical to the absorption of a tachyon with negative energy that goes forward in time (similar to the relation related to anti-matter)" (Kaku, M., Physics of the Impossible, 443)

Therefore what comes back in time is negative energy, and the source it comes back to is also filled with negative energy. Logical. This would however mean that these clairvoyants would possess a greater quantity of negative energy than the average mortal. That is, if we're to believe SF stories, of course.

....

"Don't do that!" she heard when she was about to sign the paper. It was a test they had told her.

Wearing a white coat and a hood that covered her hair completely the Asian doctor, smiling widely, had handed her the papers and had explained in general what was to happen. So convincing had she been that she had nearly signed.

"I hope you know what you are doing" she said to the doctor and noticed how the pleased expression of the doctor turned into a grin this time.

"Don't sign!" she heard again. She looked around. The only other person there was a nurse, a large, middle-aged woman that quietly hummed a song. She asked to read the paper again.

After the first lines, she stopped. A radioactive substance, sugar, would be injected in her bloodstream to be monitored, researched, and analyzed. She took one of the notebooks and searched frantically for the text she had copied from the book. It was about the experiments done on human subjects with the help of radioactive substances.

She took the papers and carefully read the text this time. When she finished, she was horrified because not only was the test dangerous, but it could have also had fatal consequences. It could have led to internal organ failure, to cardiac arrest.

In a fraction of a second she revisited the night when she had been brought into the emergency ward, when so many people had crowded around her, asking if there was anyone they could notify. She didn't want to worry anyone so she had given no names. Only now did she realize she would have been a good organ donor in case everything had failed, she would have ceased to exist. There would have been no one to claim the body.

"I have to think about it" she answered and asked to be taken back to her room. The Asian doc looked at her harshly now.

"It's okay, she has the right to read the text" the new lady doctor had said when she had come in and heard about her decision, about not undergoing the medical evaluation.

She had taken her bag and hugged it to herself as if it had been her sheet anchor. She started to shake a bit all over as if she had a fever. The young man, the same one who had brought her to the test room, had started to gently push the bed. She felt like crying and screaming, but she didn't.

The elevator door opened and two identical men appeared in the gap.

They looked at each other without a word while a crooked smile appeared on their faces. So unexpected was the image that for a moment she had forgotten all about where she was.

The man sat on the chair, beside to his mother's bed. He had shown her how to go online wirelessly. She took out the laptop and began to write. "Don't sign it!" she still heard the echo in her ears. Had it been the soul, the consciousness, or the inner self that had told her what to do?

Or maybe was it a guardian Angel?

July, at 7:02

It was after midnight. Every now and then the dogs from the sheepfold announced that an outsider was getting too close to their territory. She read:

"The patient's head is placed inside a toroid magnetic field (hmm, what could this be?). The magnetic field determines the nuclei of the atoms of the brain to align parallel to the field lines. A radio pulse is sent through the patient's body causing the oscillation of the nuclei. When the nuclei change their orientation, they emit a small radio echo which can be detected."

But then, if I had to recap, the blood sugar concentration in the human body (the radioactive sugar) would lead to the issuance of positrons, anti-electrons which the instruments would easily detect and the magnetic field makes the nuclei of the atoms in the brain to align parallel with the field lines inside your noggin while the radio pulse sent to the person's body causes an oscillation of the nuclei which change their orientation, transmitting a detectable radio echo.

Then she read:

"If the electrons are described by a wave, then what is it oscillating?"

"The NUCLEI, of course!" she said and looked as if it was the most obvious thing in the world.

The waves = equals electrons, and they seem that would cause the oscillation of the nuclei of the atoms in the brain, which then align in a certain way. How can these researchers know how the nuclei arrange? Well,that's easy. They read the pattern, they register it, read what pulses are being sent and next time, they send the same wavelength in, to obtain the same pattern".

"...and make people do as they want, controlling their actions, their minds..."

...because the brain activity is related to the oxygen consumption. The higher the concentration of oxygenated blood to the brain is, the greater the brain activity becomes. Virtually, the brain is a transmitter and by its help, the thoughts are issued in the form of electrical signals and electromagnetic waves.

What about Maxwell's laws - or what about the delayed waves, which are bundles of "advanced" fascicles, which would be nothing more than matter travelling in time creating anti-universes?

Phu, it's hard to get science. Maybe I should take some courses in physics. Quantum.

I do not think it would hurt. Not like now.

Headache pills, please!

Or about

The secret of saying and thinking

So, the thoughts are transmitted in the form of electric signals (waves) and electromagnetic waves and when a radio pulse is sent into the body, it causes its oscillation (of thinking).

I find it weird that sometimes the thought can be transformed into reality, while when we are speaking, the events would happen the other way around.

It means that the thought would consist of electric and electromagnetic waves of a certain value, characteristic, intensity and frequency, while the voice would be the thought, the same electric and electromagnetic waves, but expressed in a verbal form.

What is the Voice?

When we talk we actually transmit waves similar to the radio waves. Or perhaps just waves with impulses of a certain frequency or something like that. I am just guessing.

This would actually mean that by saying a thought out loud, you would transmit the same type of electromagnetic waves used in the process of thinking, but of opposite direction and with a reverse charge. Or perhaps, if I continued to beat around the bush, I could say that since the formation of thought and up to its verbal expression, the matter would get to travel through time into the future and would come back making the events happen in an anti-universe.

This idea (if we think about what Schrodinger was doing when he discovered this and that) occurred to me while I was eating a good trout. I was sitting at the table, having already ordered it but still waiting for it to be brought. Apropos time travelling or tachyons!

If I come to think about it, the waiter took the order, left, travelled back in time and came back in time again, with the order, a delicious trout.

Travelling back and forth in time, with the fishes.

Funny, really funny! That was a good one!

....

Back in her room, she continued to read.

It was well on in the evening when she decided it was time for a cup of tea.

The weather had been bad and the few tourists that had been there during the day, were long gone. Three men were sitting at a table reviewing the sales of the day. They threw her a quick view then continued their talk ignoring her.

The perfect combed hair was divided into two equal black sheets hanging loose over his ears too big to hide beneath the curtains of his hair. His fade grey eye bows were jumping from corner to corner of his eyes as in a frenetic Brownian movement. With a periodical movement, the tip of his tongue was following the same rhythm as his eyes, over his thin lips. From time to time he made sure his red-spotted bow tie was in place, adjusting it as if it was necessary. He held the floor. The rest of the crew, marked by the day's effort, had all indifferent and tired features and barely had the energy or dared to say a word.

When the phone rang nobody seemed to pay attention to the dialogue. She continued to enjoy her hot tea unbothered until bits of conversation made her cough in an acute, convulsive, way. Those around looked puzzled not knowing if they should intervene or not.

"The package? Okay. At ..."

She anxiously looked a few times over the shoulder towards the window behind her while with quick steps she was heading for the exit door. Something or someone had been there for a short moment. Then a flash of the two young strangers, the blonde and the young guy appeared, talking outside her door in a whisper but loudly enough so that she could hear.

"So they had come there to perform the job, to deliver the package. They were talking about a metropolis, about money. And now..."

She opened the door. The wind was blowing hard bringing strong gusts of rain. Every now and then the flash of distant lightning travelled across the sky with its glow. It was a terrifying show. She waited for the moment between two gusts and ran to her room.

Only if she had known what was about to come
Soon

....

Her head was weighing on her terribly hard and was almost throbbing. It was middle of the night. Her eyes fell on the bottle of water that was beside her bed. Just a glance as long as a second:
"Your soul saved you"

She tried to go back to sleep but the same terrible thought about what had happened during the evening lingered on. She had accidentally heard their conversation.

They held her, tied her up. A prisoner in a cage. In a town. She hadn't been able to do a thing. And all this time the people around seemed not to have known anything, or if they had known it they had tried to hide it, to forget what had happened in front of their eyes

A long Time

Desperate
Medial or medieval
A mathematical time
In an upward slope graphics
Of souls in a Brownian motion
Of coffee with sea foam
In the incandescent lights

Of a submarine volcano

Disturbed only by the innocent attempts

Of a flora and fauna of a Florentine kind

With Venetian carnival masks

And living sculptures on pedestals

Inclined, strung, astride...
Smiling
In gilded grins
Of an exaggerated protuberant white
On TV commercials

Abandoned

The Path

July, same year

"....It's not that fate is set against you. You are simply seeing reflections of your deepest beliefs, as consciousness unfolds the drama drawn up beforehand in your mind. It's the universe's task to unfold reality; yours is only to plant the seed." (Adapted from Reinventing the Body, Resurrecting the Soul, by Deepak Chopra, Harmony Books, 2009)

As soon as she woke up, she started to write. She had lunch alone on the closed terrace.

The two tourists seemed to have disappeared, and also the car which had been parked for a few days in front of her window. Modern and alert rhythms played at a high volume came from the TV placed at the entry. It didn't take long before the waiter appeared. He quietly waited. A shadow of concern fell upon his face. He took the order and vanished.

This time she had ordered trout.

....

She stopped and looked at the forest. It was comforting. The infernal noise made by the group in the room next to her could still be heard. She took off her backpack and walked a few paces. It was almost impossible to see the tops of the trees.

She closed her eyes and let herself be carried away by the discreet sounds of the rustling leaves. The fog had started to come in, creating august configurations of trees in modern graphic.

"If the hydrogen and oxygen particles emit waves of certain frequencies, just like radio waves, then, thinking about the fact that a great part of the composition of the cosmic space..."

The bright holes were staring innocently at her while the corners of its mouth rose in a playful smile. The presence was so unexpected that she didn't react. She felt how it touched her, then how it slowly merged with her body.

....

The fact that many things had happened the other way around than it had been planned or thought, was no longer a surprise to her. How it was possible and what forces controlled the result of an intention was not as easy to answer as she thought but she liked playing with ideas, with "supposing that", or "what if", and…

She took out the contents of her wallet and counted. Thirty two. Thirty two battered bills. Precisely the amount she had to pay. She burst into tears. Maybe it had all been way too much everything that she had been through, but this was too much. It wasn't the first time that this happened. She had never counted the money before and yet every time she had in her wallet no more that the amount of money that she had to pay. It was as if unknown forces made this thing happen, as if someone counted her money that she would have to get rid of it. She didn't understand how this was possible. Maybe she saw without looking. Maybe she felt without touching. Maybe

"Are you ok? Can I help you?" asked the woman that had appeared at the counter.

"No, thanks" she answered and put the bills on the counter.

Ever since she had found out about the separation she had almost stopped eating. She ate little, only as much as she needed to stay alive. She didn't know how long the money would last so every cent was counted twice to make sure that she could pay for the room. She wasn't sure where she was, in what part of the city. The internet connection had been disconnected and the map she had didn't tell her much.

That evening she ate the leftovers then tried to rest. The day had been long and tiring. She felt a sharp pain going through her chest. She took the phone and dialed the emergency number.

At 3:00 pm

"Because spirit is on the move, constantly creating your life from the invisible source of all life, you must be alert at any time to understand its ways." (Adapted after Deepak Chopra, Jan 14)

If she had been asked a question and the answer would have been "yes", then the result of the action, no matter how incredible it might seem, would be "no", the opposite. When the answer to the question would have been "no", the result of the action would have been "yes", therefore positive.

But if the answer to the question would have been probabilistic, intentional (to try) then the result could have been both "yes" and "no", positive and negative.

Consequently the axis space-time…

She had wanted an egg for breakfast.

"Do you need help?" *the waiter asked.*

"No, thank you. I think I can manage", *she answered and smiled thinking that was not such a big deal.*

The first thought had been to put the egg in the pocket, but she had put it on the plate instead, and the plate on the coffee cup. She tried to open the door without losing balance. A little inclination of the arm, then of the hand and the gravity would have done the rest. The egg smashed leaving yellow spots on the floor and on the door. If she only had concentrated on the cup instead of looking at the door

"I wonder what had made me change my mind about putting the egg in my pocket."

....

She had signed in for an exam, for a job in a big crowded city making new acquaintances, new friends. Now she was staying in an empty room all by herself, in the middle of nowhere, without meeting anybody. Without any

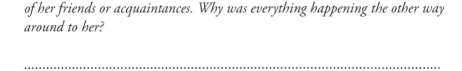

of her friends or acquaintances. Why was everything happening the other way around to her?

She gave up on eating egg that morning. She sipped the hot coffee and looked outside.

A man that she had never seen before, older than his fancy sport clothes wanted to make him look, sat at the table close to her. After exchanging glances with the newcomer, the waiter rushed to her. He was obviously disturbed by her presence:

"Is it something more, ma'am?"

"Just to return the coffee cup" she said.

The breakfast was still steaming when she got out of the salon with the tray balancing in her hands. Halfway to her room she turned her eyes towards the hut. The two hastily disappeared on the narrow trail behind the building. The plastic bag they were carrying was too heavy even for two men of their size. Suddenly the unequal mass in the bag started to move spasmodically. The tourist took out a bat and hit it hard until the movements stopped.

She slammed the door behind her. The tray with the breakfast was lying beside her, on the floor. She was staring, incapable of making any move. It was as if time had vanished.

"Did they see me? If only I had that power of thought" she said and closed her eyes. Her wide eyes searched desperately in the room after something that could have helped her. She could hardly breathe. With trembling hands she took the book and opened it randomly. She read:

"page 255, Newton's third Law - For each action there is an equal and opposite reaction!"

256. Monopoles and the Inflationary Theory

What is the thought?

She woke up in a sweat. With a quick movement of the foot, she kicked off the blanket, took off the shirt and remained lying. Almost naked. She stared at the ceiling without moving a finger. It was too hot. Early. Too quiet. She tried to go back to sleep but couldn't stop thinking of the day before. There were too many thoughts and images from that apocalyptic, twisted dream, with towns exploding and disintegrating. The rise along a wall of rock and cliffs. Enormous. Silence. Distances had become Endless. The Space, an incandescent center. Lights curving into endless limits of black holes. Flashes of winding fluids, sinuous, unseen before.

Everything was so real. Could it have been the moment when the false vacuum opened?

July Dogs

"If I met them perhaps I could ask about the dogs", she thought and continued to look over the meadow outside her door. It was only seven in the morning but the flock was already returning from pasture.

"Thinking of the "wolf", she said and rushed to meet the herd. She started to speak with the shepherd and, with no further introduction, asked if she could follow them.

It had rained all night which had made the trail slippery. Although the sheepfold was not far from her room, she managed to get wet almost up to her knees from the tall grass bordering the path.

"That's the way we milk the sheep here", said one of the shepherds as an excuse for the poor conditions while she watched how the sheep entered through a narrow gate to be milked and then go out in the pen. She felt that she had to say something, to excuse them. She told them she used to spend the holidays in the countryside and she actually knew how the sheep were milked but she had never seen the process up close. She recalled how much she liked the smell of warm, freshly milked milk, the smell of hay and was about to leave when they invited her to stay for dinner. She knew they were tired and had been up when there was still dark outside and didn't want to disturb them, but her curiosity was stronger.

"Gladly!" she replied thinking that she had passed many times a sheepfold but had never entered to see what it looks like.

The fire was burning in the middle of the room, directly on the floor. There were three beds in the narrow room placed along the walls. The solid wooden table occupied the corner that had remained open. She sat on a stool, near the fire.

"It smells so good!" she said and remembered the time when she was in the countryside and they made polenta in a pot, almost as big as this one, and they baked bread in the wooden oven in the middle of the yard. Pine wood heated up to incandescence, maize set to boil, scorching heat.

She took off her sneakers and placed them close to the fire. Wet steam started to rise from her soggy socks. Above the fire, the large cauldron for polenta was steaming homely. They gathered around the fire and the shepherds began to tell stories that had taken place years ago. When they were young.

The feast was simple. Boiled potatoes fried in oil, cucumber salad with onions and fresh cheese. In the middle, polenta! Big, golden. Steaming. For everyone. They ate in silence.

She remembered the mountain back home, the trips she used to make each weekend.

She remembered him.

....

"If I gave it something to eat, then perhaps it would follow me and I wouldn't be alone on the trail" she thought while watching the dog that stood under her window, curled, trying to warm up in the morning sun. The fog had begun to disperse.

She took the same path as the days before when she had tried to reach the ridge but after a while she realized that she was on the same trail as the small group in front of her. Without realizing it, she had followed them. To her surprise, the dog followed them too. It was not exactly what she had expected.

"A much better trail, dry too! Good to know that those guys are in front of me. Have to keep up so that I wouldn't lose them out of my sight. Alone, without a map or compass, not a good idea at all. Lucky me they are here".

The road they reached was steep and rocky. From time to time she could see the brisk tail of the dog. It hadn't left them. Near the top the fog was so thick that you could hardly decipher the contours of the trail. The group stopped to read the map.

"Think if I'll get lost! No one will find me in this fog. Maybe it's time to ask if I could follow them and keep them company."

They stopped. Looking down at the valley she had a shock. The image was incredibly similar to that from her dream. A wall of stone then the abyss.

Dark clouds rose up from the narrow valley embracing the lanky silhouettes of the trees until the edges merged and disappeared diluted.

*The height was amazing, stunning. It was like she was Space. And Time.
The thought. And the moment. The whisper. And the Touch. The breathing.
And the morning.*

As She was Everything. In that unfathomable vastness
She existed

"The gap!" she whispered and felt the void inside her, around her.
A shiver of horror passed throughout her body when she saw one of the
young men on the edge of a rock. To his right there was the gap.

She thought that she needed to do something, to make him climb
down from that place. She said something, something that sounded
rather as an invitation to come join her and watch the view, than a
warning of fear.

"Please! It's less dangerous" she whispered full of horror, of panic.

Begging

*"Could what I had seen in my dream be a prediction of what was about
to happen the next day? Could this have been the reason I have decided so
suddenly to go out on the track?"*

They reached the ridge when the clouds broke. It was warm. It was quiet. She stopped to watch. She thought about him. She thought about her.

But maybe it was something else. Maybe in the end it was all about me, about the person I was meant to be. Maybe I found a moment, that moment of serenity when reaching for the stars. With the feet on the ground.

A small spot.

A shadow

If only I could stop

Time

Still July, @: 2:25

I think I found something about magnetic and electromagnetic fields, I think it was on page 58, in the book.

In his research, Maxwell had asked himself what happened if the magnetic and electromagnetic fields were always transforming one into the other following "an endless stereotype". On page 157, it was written:

"The process of thinking actually looks like a ping-pong match played in different parts of the brain and which is triggered sequentially; the electric activity "bounces" all over the brain."

And then I asked myself:

If it was like Maxwell had said it, that the electric waves transformed into magnetic waves and the other way around, then it could have been possible that by sitting in a closed room, the simple issuance of a thought would lead, according to Maxwell's theory, to its continued repetition, the thought transforming reciprocally one into the other.

It seems that the researchers have developed a computer capable of recognizing patterns specific to the thoughts, only by using microwaves. And it also results that these microwaves play a decisive part when we move our muscles in a certain way. Interesting! Moreover, no matter how incredible it may sound like, it seems that these thoughts correspond to different patterns which are formed when the thought is issued.

....

The spoon she had held in her hand fell on the small blue carpet in the shape of a heart.

"Blue, soul, psyche, psychology. Therefore I should read psychology!"

She laid back, took another sip and waited. In a short while she should be downtown. However she continued to enjoy her coffee and let the first rays of sun caress her.

"After all I deserve this moment"

It was that feminine instinct, or perhaps from bygone genes, that made her ask herself a useless question: what to wear. It was simple: a pair of jeans and a T-shirt. Fast and easy. Convenient too.

She turned left with the intention of leaving the room but the next moment she hit her head against the closet as a reminder that she had plenty of clothes the only thing she needed to do was to open it. And choose.

"Ouch!" *she said and took a step back rubbing her forehead. She was left stunned.*

"How could something like this happen? I could have stumbled but there is no carpet on the floor, nothing to stumble upon".

A few years had passed since she had bought something for real and last time she had the chance, she had impulsively bought almost everything that had been on sale. Ever since, she had lost a few sizes and almost nothing fit her anymore.

"I should sell them" she thought, "maybe I can get a buck off of them".

She opened the door of the wardrobe, pulled out a few things and started to try them on. The last pair of jeans and a white, simple t-shirt she had bought still fit her. She descended the stairs in a hurry and rushed to the station with quick steps, almost running. She still had a few minutes until the bus would come.

....

Microwaves, something worth talking about if it was possible for thoughts to be read and decoded by a computer. If these patterns were, or are, recognized, then maybe it would be possible to use feelings for scientific or experimental purposes. Cool!

The sun hadn't come yet. The book was laying on the floor, open on the page on Maxwell's laws.

"I wonder what that guy had meant when he asked me if I knew where he could find a magnet for a person from Vienna. A magnet, a monopole. A magnet with only one pole, positive or negative. Monopoles apparently existed before the Big Bang and they had an essential role in creating the "bang".

She lay on the bed and pulled the blanket over her head. She still had a few good hours of sleep ahead of her. On the horizon a thin golden wire separated earth and sky.

Intermezzo

Summer. Time

Time mattered. Only
She felt the stomach rising and the ears clogging. She swallowed a few times.

"Only a few minutes, just a few minutes" she thought.

"Ladies and gentlemen, welcome to…"

....

The attic was large. A few wires were drawn from one end to the other of the supporting beams. She turned as if to leave but the door didn't open.

"So, they locked me in here"
She thought it was hardly the case to shout, instead she waited. Eventually they were going to discover that she was missing. She began to walk around inspecting the attic, seeking through nooks and corners. There were remnants of the earlier buildings, old shelves, metal sheets, hardware, old windows all covered with dust. In the farthest corner she found a sofa.

"If I removed the plastic and sat down, I could get some rest. It is quiet here and cool".
The thought was tempting. She looked again at the hung laundry.

"Ha, what an idea!" and hung the wet clothes again, changing their places. She noticed with astonishment that when she stood between two damp sheets, she felt different. More relaxed.

"Interesting!" she said to herself and took a few more steps.
She couldn't say exactly what the difference was but that state of relaxation had persisted. She felt, in a sense, free. She had read that water particles from the atmosphere have certain frequencies of a particular intensity, and that they are positively and negatively charged.

"Electromagnetic radiations emitted during the thought process, are also positively and negatively charged".

She recalled the day she had been on the mountain route, up in the mountain, surrounded by fog. When the air was damp and it felt good.

"If the frontal lobe would be responsible for the thought process by being the sender of radiations and the cerebellum would be the receiver, then"

She couldn't stop asking why she was feeling better when she faced the damp sheet.

"The sheet which covered a fairly large surface would have represented an area where the concentration of water molecules was much higher than around it. It is possible that the electromagnetic waves emitted had been absorbed by the water particles along with the excess energy. That resulted in the state of relaxation."

She moved the sheet again.

"How long will it take before they noticed my absence?"

....

She paused to catch her breath. She hadn't hiked in a long time and she felt the lack of exercise throughout her whole body. The dog had followed them faithfully the whole way. Whenever the small group stopped, it also stopped waiting to be rewarded. The boys were still resting. Without much thought, she took out the notebook and began writing.

"Where were the others? I should at least be able
to hear their voices", she thought.

She had remained alone when the trail began to narrow, dark and gloomy. The fog had started to lift. The vigorous trees had now been replaced by scrawny saplings frightened by their own shadows. Scenes with a solitary lost tourist, attacked by wild animals passed her mind.

"Not a good idea!" she said in a half voice to herself but loud enough to make sure that she could be heard by any wild soul that would happen to be around her at that moment. She tried to think of something else.

"What would happen if I took the notebook and wrote? Writing could help. The text maybe can make a difference"

She took out the notebook and began to write, to delete, to add, forgetting that she was alone.

"The laws of physics. What if it was possible to change them, simply by amending a text, a sentence or a tense?"

The voices were loud and clear now. They were somewhere not far away.

"Don't lose sight of them!"

Was it the consciousness?

. . . .

Discussion upon Newton's law

Coming back upon Newton's law which says that "For every action there is an equal and opposite reaction" I could say that if action would correspond to matter and reaction to antimatter, with matter meaning beams of advanced waves travelling into the future and then back in time, then it might actually mean that Newton's third law would be nothing else but an expression of the fact that antimatter, under the form of advanced beams, existed, and that time travel was actually possible. Under the shape of wave beams.

In my opinion Newton expressed the effect, but not the cause that determines the Action and Reaction to occur. That's what I think. Actually I don't know the details of the law. It's just an opinion. And since everyone has the right to an opinion

Speaking of the law of causality!

(November?)

"Ok! That's it! I'm going to call the cops" said the lady driver and stopped the bus. She took the mobile phone and dialed a number.

"Are you going to really call them?" she asked in amazement, not believing her ears.

She had only taken a few things when she fled from the place where she had been taken against her will, things she had worn every day until they began to look like rags. She really looked awful, like a street woman. Like a beggar.

It was cold, raining and the temperature had dropped to almost zero. The tank top she had put around her neck to protect from the cold, was not enough. And now the driver, a dark haired Latin American with a pageboy haircut and fine delicate features, would throw her off the bus, something she had not really understood. She was shaking. Suddenly she realized that she could actually take advantage of the situation and request the police officer to take her to the station. After all she had to get to the police station.

He was almost six feet tall albino, wearing nothing but a pair of pants, leaving in plain sight his body covered with alternating pink and light brown hue patches. She kicked him out. She had the right to privacy, she had argued as a last resort to save herself. She was angry, furious. Her reaction surprised him so much that he left without saying a word.

The police car stopped beside the bus. She thanked the driver who was completely stunned.

"Crazy woman!" the bus driver had said in a low voice but loud enough to be heard.

Thinking about how she looked she wasn't far from such an image. She was happy to see the police officer (maybe she really was "crazy" after all), and eager to tell him the whole story in short. She then asked him if he could take her to the precinct. It was his turn to be surprised:

"I can take you to the border line between the two counties. From there, it's not much further so you could take a taxi" the officer said while opening the back door of his car.

Her body was shaking like a leaf. The loose, summer clothes could hardly protect her from the cold. The wind had gotten stronger and the rain had begun to lash against her fragile body. She climbed into a police car for the very first time.

The bench was hard, cold. She was surprised to see that it was only a hard piece of plastic with nothing else on it.

"So uncomfortable!" she said to herself and for a second the idea to ask the police officer if she could sit in the front passed her mind.

"So naïve of me! So stupid! Of course it is not possible, this is not a taxi, you idiot!"

She took her bag and hugged it tightly to her chest hoping she might warm herself a little. She looked through the Plexiglas that separated her from the police officer, trying to hear what he was saying. Her thoughts were already far away.

Somewhere on a sunny beach

Notebook 2

"Experimentally we find that, indeed, the constants of nature seem to be finely tuned to allow life and even consciousness. Some believe that this is the sign of a cosmic creator. Others believe that this is a sign of the multiverse." (Kaku, M., Parallel Worlds – glossary)

"Once the counting stops, you will wake up" the man said, and then he had caught her hips and had started to pull her softly.

She was awake. Awake within her and could hear clearly what they were saying. When the count reached ten, she opened her eyes. Confused she sat on the bed. She couldn't understand what it all was about and how things happened. And wondered if she would ever understand
it

....

Or about:The Nature and Propagation of Light

"In 1873, Maxwell showed that light consists of electromagnetic waves of extremely small wavelengths and in 1887 Heinrich Hertz showed that microwaves possessed all the properties of light waves. They could be reflected, refracted, focused by lenses, polarized and so forth, same as light waves." (Physics, Chapter 38, 624)

So this would mean that each color of the light spectrum by having a specific wavelength (frequency) could give rise to certain cerebral processes at micro level, turning into, or giving birth to certain thoughts or images, thus changing the way in which we perceive reality. Maybe this explains how and why different colors influence what we feel and how we react

....

She had packed a few things in a hurry, while the car was waiting at the gate, much too flimsy for the mountains:

"In fact, they would be more appropriate for the beach. Why am I packing such things? I have no idea"

The room was bright and spacious. She threw the things on the bed without worrying about whether or not they were dry. Then for a moment she looked at the pile of clothes spread chaotically. She looked again. She took two steps toward the door and stopped. At that moment she understood why she had packed them. It had nothing to do with the weather, or with the fact that they were too flimsy. Or with their texture. It was about the colors.

On 23th of…, at 7:00 pm

I had an idea. What if these advanced waves travel through time, scan the future light years away and return all of a sudden to let us know that in fact the impossible is possible? This could mean that time travel would be possible, although not as we imagined it traditionally in SF movies, by the "physical" transportation of the matter, but as forecasts, as precognition.

On Temporal Quasi Curves

....

@:7:47 pm.

It seems that Einstein's equations gave birth to many types of time machines. Today I found in my little travel book something interesting about The Temporal Quasi Curves, the technical term for paths that allow for time travel into the past. It says:

"If we followed the path of a closed quasi temporal curve, we would set out on a journey and return before we left" (Kaku, M., The Physics of Impossible, 362)

After reading this, I was haunted by a thought. A silly one, but nonetheless.

The trip on Sunday, two weeks ago, right before I came out of the house, between taking two steps toward the door, I thought about taking the key and the wallet. I wonder how long did it last. A second? A split second? And if so, the soul, or maybe the consciousness, would be matter traveling through time knowing what would happen to me, and told me what to do, then WOULDN'T THAT MEAN THAT I TRAVELED THROUGH TIME according to Einstein's theory?

On a quasi-temporal curve, on a closed quasi-temporal curve. Quick enough as a thought.

Two steps. While I was in the past, still in the house which in fact was "the present" (so inappropriate to use "was" together with "present", totally non-sense, or maybe not), and returning before I left.

Confused? Some of you. Okay, let me explain.

What I mean is that my inner self – the advanced waves, reached the place where we were going to meet, saw what happened and returned to tell me that I should take the key and the wallet. Otherwise I would have walked allllll the way home and who knows how long it would have taken me.

Taking into account the fact that these advanced beams would be, if I'm right, emitted by my own body, part of the matter which constitutes me, then this would mean that I simply did a "little" time travel!

In conclusion, I could PROUDLY state that I have demonstrated through this little discussion that Einstein's law on time travel by means of quasi temporal curves is real!

....

8:02 PM

If we were to follow the path of a closed quasi-temporal curve, "we would start a journey and return before we left," said the scientist.

Kurt Gödel, another smart guy, found the first solution to Einstein's equations on time travel. He said that if the universe rotates and we would travel around it fast enough, then we could find ourselves in the past and we would return before we left. Or something like that.

Brilliant!

And now returning to my fantastic On Topic Discussions, reviewing, I would say that:

If the universe is spinning and if I traveled around the universe fast enough, I could be in the past and I could return before I left, as already shown. So, recap, this would mean that, according to my assumptions that the soul is matter traveling in time, I have demonstrated that time travel on a closed quasi-temporal curve wave (according to Einstein) is possible. And that the universe rotates (as Kurt Gödel assumed).

In other words I took a spin on a closed quasi-temporal curve around the universe that rotates, because I was fast enough to return before I left. And smart girl,I took the keys and the wallet.

Funny! Cool! ME and the UNIVERSE!

I don't know what I ate but...
It could be that advanced wave beam ☺

26th of…, at 10:13 AM

I had another flash, one of those "Aha!" moments, as Guru said. By the way, I wonder what he's doing. I wrote to him but he never answered back. I wanted to have a little chat with him about soul and stuff like that. I wonder what he would have said. Maybe it wasn't meant to be. Maybe next time. May I'll have a better luck with the mathematician.

But what was I talking about? Aha, about the "AHA!"s. You know when you suddenly realize something or an unexpected idea comes to mind and you go "AHA!"

I was thinking about that time when I had a thought, or an idea (actually ideas are thoughts as long as they are not expressed), about situations or people that could protect you from all and everything in the world around, and I burst into laughter as I hadn't in a long time, because it seemed soooo impossible. Sooo crazy! That flash that came out of nowhere, who knows, maybe it will come true one day. It was a moment I enjoyed enormously. Funny! Funny! Twice today

In fact why not?

Then, in a blink of an eye, the thought took shape. At that moment, she decided to leave.

....

She was sitting on the floor in the empty room surrounded by papers and a few things she could grab when she left in hurry. She used to sleep in one of the corners, covering her with the only thing she had, a blouse with long sleeves. The rest of her belongings she put in a t-shirt and used it as a pillow.

It was a long time since she had a proper meal. The things that happened over the last few days made her even thinner. Several times she tried to contact the man but no one answered.

She looked again at her hand, at her fingers. The skin had become so thin that the veins colored in dark blue and purple were clearly visible now. They were showing up like rivers running through the hills and valleys of that hand. Her hand. So thin, so strong.

So powerful
She looked outside. The first snow was falling down.
It was November.

28th of…, at 12:45

Subject: The Fourth Stage of Love: Intimacy

"The law of intimacy states that in true intimacy flesh merges with flesh, and spirit with spirit. In intimacy, sexual energy and spiritual energy are recognized as one. Sexual energy is seen as the creative energy of the universe" (Adapted from the Kama Sutra by Deepak Chopra, Virgin Books, 2006)(Chopra, The Kama Sutra, 2006)

Speaking of the mathematics of love!

If sexual energy is seen as spiritual energy, and spiritual energy would be the same thing as the soul, this would mean that while making love, a release of energy would take place in the form of gamma radiation that would result in from the collision of positive and negative electrons.

I know you are raising an eyebrow right now wondering what the heck this is all about, questioning maybe my fantastic conclusions. But be patient! Take a walk, take a thought, take a kitkat (only if you want to) and …relax.

That night on the beach...

They were near the sea. She looked in the distance. Or nearby

"Fertilize the ocean!" she found herself saying while she was letting the few drops on her fingers disappear in the sea foam.

He stood a few steps behind her. She didn't turn around but felt him watching her.

"Really strange things happen when I'm around you" she heard him saying, almost like a whisper, most to himself.

The water was almost up to the ankles. Without hesitation she pulled of the flimsy blouse which covered her frail body. She closed her eyes and stood like that, naked and without saying a word. A few months ago she had imagined that she was making love by the sea under a starry sky.

It had become true. She should have understood long ago that everything was possible, that she could see into the future.

Laying on the hot sand, embracing each other, they were looking at the sky:

"I haven't been at the sea side so late in a very long time.
It's quite romantic" he said and hugged her.

"Did you see that? A shooting star!" he said excited, and looked at her with an imperceptible smile on his face.

"Yes!" she had replied and saw how for a moment the man beside her was turning into the child he had been many years ago, happy to see a shooting star.

"Did you make a wish?" she had asked him turning toward him and watching him more or less playfully to see what he was going to say.

"Maybe" he murmured.

She let her head back:

"Look! Upside down"

Everything was upside down. The beach, the ocean and the sky were upside down.

The sky had turned into an ocean. The ocean was the sky.

And the beach

And the Earth

The beach was just a thin line separating the two worlds from each other, from themselves, allowing them to float in the cosmic vastness of interstellar dreams. The Earth was resting on her shoulders, letting her carry the entire burden of a world unknown, untold before.

A parallel world

"You could really stay here forever, couldn't you?" he had asked her and gently kissed her lips.

It was exactly what she had thought a moment before.

"Yes" she had answered without being surprised by the fact that he had guessed her thought. She closed her eyes and felt his arms around her. He kissed her lingeringly:

"Do you think someone saw us?"

"I don't know. Does it matter? Maybe one or two satellites" she answered and they both burst into laughter.

....

The fact that I met him again would not be a coincidence if it hadn't been as it was, with everything that's happened. With all the time traveling. The soul. The consciousness. The equations. He.

Who is HE? Embodied divinity, the He that I had to meet and fall in love with? Or maybe

Her feet were sinking deeply into the wet sand. The warm foamy waves were rushing over her ankles, soaking the hem of her pants. She was walking without looking. Only the ocean had fascinated her. She had wanted to see the beach, the waves. The seagulls. To feel the air of the distances. Of the depths. She had contemplated the smooth flight of the seagulls gliding at the mercy. At that moment she had been free, without fears or worries. Like a seagull.

"So do you think you could prove that you love your kid?" he asked.
"Yes, I do"
"How?" he continued watching a spot on the horizon.
"I am here"

He looked at her surprised. They continued to walk on the beach without saying a word. From time to time their shoulders touched involuntarily making them aware of the other one's presence.

The people, the beach, the distance and the close, disappeared.

All that remained was the thought.

29th of…, at 4:00 PM

Subject: the meaning of sex

Do you remember when I wondered in one of my emails about the significance of sex?

Today I received an email that says love is, or could be, the guiding principle in the universe.

Guiding principle?

Come on!

However, if the situation hadn't been as it was, and if it hadn't been for the desire to understand what was going on, then nothing of what happened so far would have been possible. Maybe someone or something, maybe the soul, took care of it all. It had arranged everything so that they would meet.

And yet, if I hadn't been so irritated by his question or by his claim that I don't want to talk to Him, then none of what I wrote would have been written or said. Or expressed, or thought. Nothing would have happened.

You asked me once if I had an answer to every question. I don't know yet.

What about you?

What would be your answer if I asked you?

....

Still 29th, at 11:15 PM

To: me

Subject: A Gift of Insight from Sound

"When I asked him what he did for a living, the man waved his hand and said: "Oh, a little healing, a little psychic stuff. You know, mind-reading. I do not pay much attention to it." (Adapted from Deepak Chopra (Three River Press, 2004)

Or about: Research and Science

Not long ago they had had an interesting discussion about species in general, about how the organisms were selected to be on the endangered species lists. It was pretty interesting.

"If organizations, whatever they may be, would be interested in protecting the species*, she said,* how come is it that viruses and bacteria responsible for diseases, were not included on the endangered lists? Who decides which of the organisms have priority on the famous list?"

"After all, if I remember correctly, *she said,* the first organisms that appeared on earth in the primordial soup were bacteria and viruses. Why should they be excluded from the list?"

"Because the decisions are taken at political level" *the answer came from someone in the group.*

"I see. But then one could ask how free science is" *she replied more for herself and lifted her head a few inches in an attempt to see the man that came with the answer.*

Then one day, long after you had returned, someone said:
"You are thinking too loud!"
Then everything changed for me.

....

"He definitely didn't take me seriously" *she thought, or maybe my email never reached its destination.*

She really wanted to meet guru and ask if he could explain what was happening and why. Perhaps he didn't take her seriously when she wrote to him that she had "time-space" issues. She imagined herself talking to him in his office. Or maybe outside, by the sea. On a deserted beach.

Only She and He

She imagined herself what he would say. What he would do.

"He would take you into an exotic world, unseen until then. The world of soul"

That day I compared the Earth to an organism and us with viruses and bacteria present in the organism. These viruses and bacteria normally coexist inside the body, as research shows, in a civilized manner, without complications. When changes occur in their environment, they weaken the host body leading to its death and finally to their own death. They kill themselves.

If scientists, by changing the existing information in viruses DNA with a more "intelligent" one making them "conscious" of their fatal end, then it could be possible to ensure a peaceful coexistence of the human body and these "bad virus & bacteria - guys". Therefore it could be possible to change or even stop the evolution of certain diseases as cancer.

What is the cell?

....

The 2ⁿᵈ, following month, at 3:☺ PM

Subject: light sources

"All bodies emit electromagnetic radiation due to thermal motion of molecules; this radiation called thermal radiation is a mixture of radiations of different wavelengths." (Physics, page 625)

The man was sitting on the beach near the water.He was looking at the surfers. Or perhaps at the heavy clouds hanging over the skyline.

Maybe he was watching the lacy waves getting closer and wetting his feet. The air was humid, heavy laden with the salt of the disheveled depths. Not long ago it had rained leaving the beach deserted. A thin mist rose above the sea, welding all the lines together.

The creature had been watching him since he had arrived on the beach and sat down. It had carefully gotten closer to him, surrounded him little by little, and smelt him. It stood up on its back paws leaning on his back. Had he ever been aware of the being that came near him? It had circled him again, had smelled his hands trying to catch his look and understand if he would ever hurt her. With its little tongue it licked him on his cheek as a sign of acceptance and trust. They stood side by side, looking into the distance, close and yet far away from each other. Worlds and words were separating them.

The sun had begun to appear from behind the clouds. In a little while it was going to disappear under the skyline.

She dove into the sea and let herself float with the waves. She was alone with a man who had told her that he found her a bit strange, unusual. The jeans were already wet almost up to her knees, so why not? Who would have cared? No one. She let the waves to breeze over her face, over her thoughts.

Sky
Clouds
Seagulls

What are the seagulls doing now?

....

2:10 AM

"Please, help me!" she asked him.

Of course she had herself to blame for not being happy, she had thought so many times without much concern to what was going on around her.

She had no clue where she was. She cried her heart out frightened to find out that he had brought her to his place, then fell asleep with her clothes on, on what once was a golden brown floral sofa now covered with big greasy spots.

Piles of dirty clothes were lying scattered everywhere among old newspapers, shopping bags and a mix of new and old, sharp, smelly tattered loafers and sandals in size - enormous. Everything looked grey, misty as if thick smog never left the room.

"You should see the client! She's hot but she's in pretty bad shape" he said. She heard him like in a dream talking on the phone. He began to laugh throatily. At the other end of the line the voice made him laugh even louder. She continued to cry silently, then began to throw up. Cramps began to torture her stomach and intestines. Everything was torn inside, feverish. She closed her eyes and waited.

"How could I end up here?"

Fri, 13th of…, at 11:35 AM

To: ME

Subject: your very own epiphany

"The value of an epiphany doesn't lie just in some new and exciting insight. You might be walking down the street and pass by a stranger. Your eyes meet, and for some reason there is a connection. It isn't sexual or romantic or even a suspicion that this person could mean something in your life. It's the sudden expansion that counts" (Adapted from The Book of Secrets by Deepak Chopra, 2004)(Chopra, The Book of Secrets, 2004)

She had met him that very morning. It was cloudy, grey and cold. It was summer. A little before they should have met, he called to say he was going to be late.

"What does he look like? Would it make any difference?" she said and looked outside through the window for the second time.

"After all, he is only going to show me the surrounding "sight-seeing" this week-end"

Tiny, warm droplets of water began falling. From far away she saw the cathedral erecting its shape. Seen from that perspective, it looked like a fortress hard to conquer. She thought of Shakespeare, of Hamlet.

Before the week-end, G. had phoned her and asked her what they were going to do. Then he told her:

"You are a big girl, you can handle it. If something does not look right, do as your intuition tells you to. And don't forget, there are more foreign students here than you can ever imagine"

"What did G. mean by that?"

The moment when she was about to enter the church, she looked back instinctively. For a moment she thought she hallucinated but the tomb's door opened and a wave of heat, smoke and a heavy putrid smell started to spread around. A hand, thin and small, showed up through the opening. She didn't tell him anything about it; instead she rushed into the cathedral.

Hidden behind the statue of Virgin Mary, the inscription on the wall was barely visible. She stopped and tried to read.

The cold breathing on her neck made her bounce aside a step.

She turned a bit and looked back hoping to see him. The place on the bench where he sat a few moments ago, holding his hands together as he was praying, was empty. He was nowhere. Vanished! Disappeared! Bum, gone! Just like that.

"What on earth is happening here? Where is he?"

She turned around. The shadow was so close to her that she found it hard to breathe. She felt how the grey smoke cloak was wrapping her, suffocating her. She opened her mouth but no sound came out. Her legs were like stone rooted in the floor. She couldn't hear anything else other than the heartbeats. Her eyes, wide opened, were desperately trying to find him. She needed him. Badly!

The rain was still falling like a fine, warm vaporous curtain. The passers-by, most of them tourists, seemed not to notice the weather. She could not help f thinking of what she had seen in the cathedral.

That figure. It reminded her of something. Or someone. She had seen that figure before.

But where?

....

The small town, a few hundred years old, was stylish like a valuable miniature. The vintage, the art and fashion boutiques, all in old style, were scattered all over the village.

The poster written in garish colors, hung by only one thumbtack. The bottom part, torn into small pieces, was laying on the ground. She read the text loud:

"The book" and "Writing"

It didn't make any sense. Suddenly it all came clear; she understood the cause of so many things. Everything had an explanation. Someone said something behind her but she did not listen. He was waiting for her a few steps away.

"Perfect! Just the two of us" she said and looked around.

The place they entered seemed deserted. They took the table next to the window hoping someone would show up soon. She looked at him from the corner of her eyes

"What could he be thinking of me?" she thought.

"I really don't understand. It looks as if people rushed to leave this place" he said and a shadow of anxiety passed over his face otherwise quiet.

"How is it possible that in such a busy town, with so many tourists, no one is here? The only thing alive is the football match on TV" he said.

"You told me that the town is known as a gay community. So interesting! I have never been in such a place. So unique! And picturesque! Yet, I wouldn't see much of those walking on the street and, as a matter of fact, I would not see any difference", she said and looked at him and over his shoulder pretending that she didn't hear his comment.

She was much more interested in what had happened at the church. About him.

"In the mountain, at the hut!" she suddenly cried so loud that he turned his head surprised.

Now she remembered. It was that night, at the hut in the mountain, when she saw the figure. He appeared as a shadow in the middle of the storm and vanished as quickly as he appeared. Could it... No sooner had she finished her thought when the door that separated the bar from the back part of the restaurant, creaked. At the same time the front door opened. A sweet choking smell crept into the room:

"That smell..." she whispered and felt that hair-raising sensation and cold chills down her spine.

She grabbed his hand and held it tightly. He looked at her unable to understand what was happening. Opened his mouth to say something.

7th of.., at 10:34AM

About Absorption

"No material is perfectly transparent, when light passes through an optic environment (except void) the energy is partially absorbed, raising the internal energy of the object (of the environment) and the intensity (power per unit area) is properly diminished." (Fizica, Page 633) (Sears)

Question: Could a light beam "bend" as if it could see round the corner?

I read the index of refraction for quartz: 1,544. So, the index of refraction of quartz being 1, 544 could deviate the frequency issued by the environment, couldn't it? And I went on: NaCl - salt - 1, 544, Ice - 1, 309, Water - 1, 330 and quartz.

This would mean that the body's index of refraction could alter according to what we eat, inflecting the U.V. light from the environment.

As all objects issue electromagnetic radiations as a consequence of the thermic movement of the molecules, it would mean that the human body would make an important source for the emission of heat into the atmosphere, with consequences on the environment. Maybe it would be necessary a certain control of the population anyway.

Poor cows! They are accused of destroying the ozone layer. What a life.

When she got to the crossroads, she stopped. Had she taken the road from the right she would have been closer to the peak of the hill. The road from the left, with a name that made her think of a wolf, she assumed it would take her somewhere in town. It would have been wonderful and tempting to see lights of the city from the top of the hill, from above, but in the last moment she decided to take the road that led to downtown.

Sitting on its back paws, the wolfhound waited. It was at the end of the street, just after she turned the corner, when she saw it. It was a stray dog that was looking for a place to sleep. Maybe it waited for a friend to give it a meal, or just to keep it company.

The 20th, at …

"The wave is a disturbance of a state of balance which moves or propagates in time from one region of space to another." (Fizica, 360)

So if I have to review, the longitudinal waves in air form sound sensations (p.368), the ear is sensitive to frequencies from 20 to 20000 Hertz, the light waves have the same character as radio waves, infrared waves, X rays and Gamma rays (p.360), all matter exhibits wave-like properties, a fascicle of electrons is reflected by a crystal (quartz, salt) and also by an X ray, mechanical waves propagate through a material environment as it alters its own state of balance.

In this way it could be explained…

"How do I know I have a soul? You cannot know by seeing it or touching it. Your soul might whisper to you, but even then you could just be hearing echoes of your own voice." (Adapted after Deepak Chopra)

She remembered the evening on the parking lot where she used to train, the moment when she started running. Fast. Strong. How all her thoughts, all the images, broke down as a mirror pulverized in a thousand pieces.

They had been to the beach and the salty air of the sea made them hungry. It was her turn to pay. The only table left free in the far back of the restaurant was covered with a red tablecloth. White plastic cutlery was laying on yellow-green striped napkin folded like a star.

She started to tell him about books, music, about travelling. And watched how he listened to her patiently, without interrupting.

"How can I find out the kind of person he is, if he's not saying a word?" she thought and took another slice of pizza.

"Do you go to the gym?" he asked her without lifting his look, busy with his slice. She felt flattered by the question:

"No. Not really"

"Taking into consideration the fact that man becomes interesting after turning 40, and a woman is always 25..." she thought and looked at him. He was over 40 and interesting. True.

A subtle smile enlightened her face. She cleared the crumbs from the table and rolled them in the napkin in her hand. She grabbed the last pizza slice and took another bite. Spots of grease started to go down her chin and fingers, towards her wrist. He gave her a napkin. She felt so embarrassed that she didn't dare to look at him.

If matter (the body included) has wave-like properties and the movement of the waves inside an environment is made with defined speed, knowing the frequency/the speed of movement of certain waves within a certain type of matter, for example the body, then sound sensation can be explained, the human ear being sensitive to frequencies ranging from 20Hz (17m) to 20.000 Hz (7cm).

The 21th, 7:29

"Seekers are those who try to solve the seeming paradox of God's indifference and God's love. This enigma is worth devoting one's whole lifetime to solving." (Adapted after Deepak Chopra)

Or on: The Molecular Nature of Gas

As we all know, gas is made of thermally agitated molecules separated by great distances compared to their diameters. We also know that the vibrations that form a wave inside a gas overlap with the thermal agitation."In the case of atmospheric pressure, the average freeway is about 10-5 cm, while the amplitude due to a weak sound can represent the ten thousandth part of it. A volume element of gas, where a sound wave is propagated, can be compared to a swarm of mosquitoes, a swarm that has slow oscillations, as a whole, while the insects apparently move randomly inside it" Found this last piece of info in the physics book, on page 368.

And moving further on a similar subject, and since I have nothing else to do and am soooo bored, I could easily say that an alien could have the following recipe: one part antimatter, (methane) gas or maybe U.V. light, microwaves, liquid in the form of hot water vapors, maybe metal, or metal ions.

It should also contain something solid otherwise we could not shake hands with them, something plastic (molecules of... I don't know what. I'm a mess at Chemistry!), detergents of course, not that they are not clean, just in case... (Insufferable Chemistry!), photons, a carcass to protect them from the outside radiations, from the composition of the atmosphere and something in its head.

Maybe a "swarm of mosquitoes" mixed up with a pinch of consciousness and a great deal of humor because you need a lot of humor to be on this planet.

Yep, definitely something in its head!

And, as they came from the future, then they would have opposite electric charges from the one with whom they shake hands, and then...

Bang!

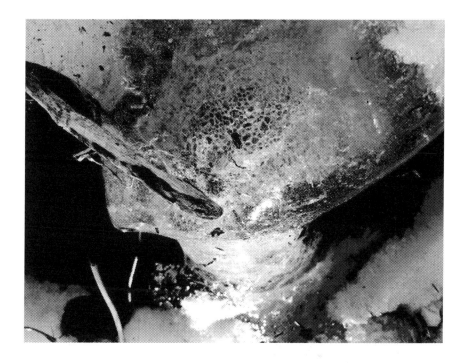

I do not know how Big but it would certainly go Bang.

7:44

Subject: Acoustic Phenomena

"When the longitudinal waves from the air come in contact with the ear, auditory sensations are formed." (Physics, page 389)

"The term of auditory intensity refers to the sensation inside the human consciousness" says the book of Physics of course. This would mean that each person has a certain point of auditory sensitivity where the sound waves of different intensity are, or are not, sensed with a specific intensity. That would mean that hearing is pure and simple a totally private and personal thing...

She finished writing her text. And read:
"I was surrounded by shepherd dogs, but strangely I was calm, peaceful. I felt safe with them."

The person entered the room. He was irritated for some reason and started a conversation with no reasonable point. So absorbed was she with her thoughts that she didn't pay him any attention. Then all unfolded so unexpectedly, even pleasantly. She remembered the day up in the mountain when lying on the grass she looked around and all she could see was sheep and shepherd dogs. How she felt safe.

"Maybe in that moment, my soul has scanned the future up until now and went back to the sunny day at the hut when I was lying in the grass, enjoying the smell of wild flowers"

Well, everything is relative

About nothing

She would often get up at about five in the morning. Now it was eight o'clock and still in bed. She packed and called a taxi. Those in the room were watching TV, completely absent-minded when she passed by them.

"Could they not notice me? How strange! What's wrong with these people?" *she thought.*
"They all looked as if having been being hypnotized, like zombies", *she said to herself as she got in the car.*
Then she left.

· ·

Seeing him she felt some kind of relief.
She really wanted to see meet him again, to talk to him. And He came. For a short time a lot of memories came through her mind. It was like a time window re-opened. She tried to understand if she was happy in that moment. She did not doubt for a moment that his embrace was honest but a strange feeling stopped her from being totally honest with him.

"I will tell you more about me" *she said, while unfolding in a few short sentences what had happened during those years that they had not seen each other. The tone of the discussion was cold and reserved:*
"It's not necessary, they have told me everything about you" *he went on with his thought, while telling her in the usual manner about his latest events.*
If up to that point she was not sure of it, now she realized what had been so weird with that place; there was only one man sitting at a nearby table, the rest were women. Silent..
The surreal scene gave her the creeps:
"They look as if they were not humans, and then the silence. It is strange that it's so quiet. In an airport?"

Mirrors

The girl from the counter desk got surprised, then indignant. When it was her turn, she got almost angry. She took a few steps backwards and nearly fell on her back, stopped by the bag left behind her.

Only a few centimeters away an older couple were talking in a low voice, absorbed by their own conversation. The girl at the desk was trying in vain to tell them they were too close to the marked line and they should not pass it. Suddenly the conversation turned into a quiet finger-hand dialogue.

For a moment it seemed that her bag disappeared from sight. She had laid the bag at her feet, and now it was almost behind her, close to the couple's big brown bag. Was she just imagining?

She heard her name called at the desk so she stepped forward. Without hesitating, the old lady opened the bag, laid the package in and closed it with same handiness as she opened it. Fast and quiet. With the tip of her shoe she pushed the bag back into its place then with a crooked smile on her face she continued to talk with her old companion as if nothing had happened.

"It's not my turn yet and the bag is in the place, so I have nothing to fear" she thought and felt more relaxed.

With one of the sandals in her hand and the belt around her neck, she almost dragged the half hanging bag on the floor. Jumping on one leg she kept on dressing all the way to the boarding gate.

The bald guy with dark sunglasses accompanied her all the way. Only a few steps behind. He said something. She put her bag on the other shoulder hoping she could see if he was talking to her or on his cell phone. The only thing she saw, from the corner of her eye, was the square, filthy leather suitcase chained to his wrist. And the shadow.

She took several deep breaths. The airplane had already started to take off.

Some time ago, @...2:23

"I am not the universe; the universe is in me…" (Deepak Chopra)

The stars filled the sky. She stopped to look at them. The evening spread the delicate fragrance of the newly opened cherry blossoms. Far away the city lights blinked like fireflies. It was so tempting.

"So far but still so close" she said.

"What are all those people doing there, at this hour? They are strolling, eating or making love probably. Maybe they are just watching a bad movie on TV, or walking on streets or parks".

She lifted her eyes.

"I wonder what it's like up there. It looks as if it is very quiet. Is it quiet? Do stars talk to each other? What could they be saying? They seem so small and so insignificant"

"Why would I be interested in stars? Once, somebody promised to show me the stars and teach me their names. It did not end up like that".

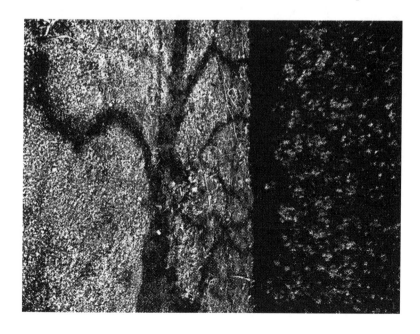

She looked more carefully at one of the stars. The four stars made up a rhomb. The fifth, barely visible, was placed in the middle. The air started to vibrate. She couldn't move. She couldn't say a word. Down, a sky of stars. Above, sky of stars. Two mirrors, one reflection.

Everything became everything. And everything was unified in only one simple existence. In two parallel worlds

....

The 27th, at 5:61

"All the atoms of our bodies are debris of that titanic clash between matter and antimatter. This theory allows the possibility that small amounts of antimatter could occur in a natural way." (Kaku, M., The Physics of Impossible, page 305)

"When did that star arise? And when did it die? Did it really die?" She kept on watching the sky. It was almost summer TIME.

The loud-speaker's voice made her startle. She had dozed off. She took the blanket from the nearby chair and covered herself hoping she would fall asleep. She had a long day, and now the flight, so many hours.... The screen began to scroll data about the distance to the destination, the altitude, speed, temperature.

"Why were we coming from Alaska?"

Origin

"What is the antimatter? It seems strange that nature should have doubled itself the number of subatomic particles in the universe without good reason. As a rule, and if the matter exists, there may be anti-universes?" (Kaku, M., Physics of Impossible, 309)

She locked the door lest she should be disturbed.

"Use the books!" she thought and like other times, she piled the books, one above the other, making a miniature chair. She felt tired and unclean. Undressed to the waist, she remained like that, half naked, without moving, until she no longer could feel her legs and arms. The body temperature dropped leaving a feeling of emptiness. She had been looking in the mirror, staring at her image:
"No past, no future. Just ME", she said.

The feeling of disappearance, of being somewhere else in another space, was too intense. She grabbed the sink and leaned over it so much that her nose touched the mirror. She could feel it. It was cold and slippery. She watched how her image disappeared behind the mist of her breathing. It was not possible to just simply vanish in another space.
For how long had she been there? The walls were covered with cold, impersonal tiles. The light, only a spot in the left corner, was strong enough to illuminate the room.

"Pottery tiles, of course! That makes sense"

. . . .

"The Space – Time dimension" she said. "What was it all about?"
The room was grey and almost empty. She looked toward one of the room's corners.
"The X, Y, Z axes!"

She was in the tridimensional space.

"Spaces. X, Y, Z. and THE ORIGIN! They were three. What about Time, the fourth dimension? You can see, touch and feel the space", she thought and let the hand slip over the cold tile.

"And Time? Can you feel it, see it and put it on the same axis of coordinates as physical dimension? But suppose we thought of quantum level, how would we represent Time? At quantum level there should be neither more nor less than eleven dimensions. Which of them would represent Time? One axes system with ten, no- eleven, dimensions. Or was it fourteen?"

And she continued:

If time were…, if Time were, for example, what we live every day, then Time would be nothing more than a notion, an expression of biological processes that occur every day in Newtonian perspective. The Action and Reaction. But what about the micro - quantum level, what would Time represent when talking about the matter and the antimatter level?

When you are in a limited space, within an isolated system then…

I wonder how I could experience the four dimensions. I could see and feel the space, being grey, bright, and cold. But Time? Considering matter and antimatter, what would have happened if I had stood there, in a relative, einsteinian silence with the four dimensions? Would it be possible that the four coordinates system, of the four (relative?) dimensions, to get to a new state of equilibrium? In this case Time is only a measure to restore the state of equilibrium. That would mean that what had happened

Before

TIME

If we considered Time not only as a concept or as a measure of biological processes, but also as a measure of the geological and geochemical processes, this would actually mean that Time IS matter. Matter in a metamorphosis that takes place at macro and micro level. At quantum level. And therefore it is SPACE, possible to be represented in an axes system.

So Time is a notion and a measure that describes matter transformation, and can be represented in an axes system. And due to the fact that we are the embodiment of matter, it means that each of us should be, no- IS, a representation of time in a space which is more or less defined.

If the conscience were indeed antimatter having the power of scanning the future or the past, giving us information about what would happen then we could consider that, what we call conscience might be the same thing as Time.

In this case conscience, the antimatter, would be responsible for the transformation of the matter at different levels.

Time would be the matter itself, and antimatter, which is auto adjusting, looking for a point within itself for the balance of the system. And we call it Destiny.

....

She had put the clothes on the back of the couch. So vitiated the air was that red spots started to appear all over her body. She felt she was choking.

The dress with thin strips of such a deep blue that it seemed almost black had white dots creating the impression of snowflakes in the middle of the night. It seemed a weird choice for a summer dress even though she had bought it. She looked at the folds that had been formed when she threw it randomly on the dirty couch, altogether with the other few things which she had bundled in hurry before she left. She remained still for a moment surprised by the thought that had crossed her mind.

"Suppose what surrounds us was information having the shape of strings which were formed by ones and zeroes, and suppose the matter and the antimatter that surround us were precisely this information, then time wouldn't be anything else but INFORMATION, information travelling in a multitude of ones and zeroes, or maybe strings of DNA. If this information was not only ones and zeroes, but strings of DNA as well, then..."

She began coughing convulsively without being able to stop. She had to drink water. She took a glass and opened the tap. Big kitchen bugs started to run chaotically visibly disturbed by the unexpected cold water. She began scratching the place where red spots had appeared a few days earlier.

The 28th ...and a half

Subject: The ionized particle and gamma radiation

She looked out through the oval window admiring the vastness of space. They were at over ten thousand feet altitude.

"How would it be to be outside, in outer space? Where is the sun right now? Certainly above us. I wish I could see it even for a second. At this altitude, with all that radiation from space" and scarcely had she thought about it when a red light beam crossed off the space landing on the magazine that she was holding and vanished as quickly as it had appeared. She was astonished.

"Was it one of those particles radiating from space that enter through everything, even the metal of a space ship? The altitude was too low and the lights from the plane were off."

She continued to watch the sky. At that height the horizon seemed to be curving in a visible way.

The man in the front seat was massaging his wrists in a rhythmic way.

"Not a bad idea. Maybe I should try it" then she felt how the plane changed its position and then slowly it made a sensitive, almost imperceptible, lean. For a moment the sky turned into a bright blue. A powerful light appeared out of nowhere.

"Look! The Sun!" she said.

She wanted to see the Sun and the wish came true. Everything seemed so strange, so incredible, and so true. All that had happened before was at that moment just history. Valueless. Everything was focused as if it had merged right in time, at that second, at that point in space. For a brief moment she had a dream. For a brief moment everything was confirmed. Out there, in space.

....

Probably the same Day

I wrote about: *The secret of the speech, of the thought, of the word*

Strange to say it but these are different things. It would seem that
the result of an action would depend in an unjustifiable way on how the
intention would be expressed; thought, said, or written.

Fascinating, isn't it?

But everything becomes even more fascinating when talking about
Thoughts and Tachyons, about the Voice. Not that radio station, of
course. Just joking.

so

If tachyons, as they say in science fiction stories, could be used for
sending messages back in time for clairvoyants then ...

Damn it! Where was I? Okay, now I know. Back from the beginning.

Feinberg believed that "the emission of a tachyon that moves forward
in time is identical with the absorption of tachyon in time." As far as I'm
concerned, from my point of view and based on my very own, personal
experience, I believe that

If

The Thought could be given in the form of electromagnetic waves of
a certain intensity and frequency, representing a means of transmitting
information, meaning emission of tachyon (if they really exist), and The
Voice would be a process where the tachyons are absorbed, having an
opposite sign then we could say that within the process of thinking, when
the thought is issued the result would indicate the tachyons emission
(matter), while in the process of issuing information with your voice,
would mean tachyons absorption (antimatter), the tachyons having in this
case a negative energy.

So, the verbal expression of a thought would be an informational
process where tachyons are transmitted and received. Thought would
represent sent information by the releasing of tachyons, and receiving
information by Voice would be the absorption of negative energy
tachyons.

....

She had begun to listen more carefully. The conversations were in the same language that she should have known, but in a strange way she had not managed to decipher a word.

She remembered when she had tried to translate a text a few years ago. "What would it be if there were phones with an instantaneous translation from one language to another? You would speak your language and the other one would speak his, and the phone software would translate both languages instantly helping people understand each other on the spot. It would be cool!" she exclaimed.

The stewardess showed up again. She looked at her inquiring, trying to tell her something. Then she handed her a pen with a name on it:
"It's my hotel"
"Thank you!" she answered watching her moving away.
"How many hours will it take until we reach the destination?"

The night at the hotel, before her leaving, she had slept only a few hours. The thoughts drove her back to what had happened in that day, to that man's interesting way of driving her to the airport, to the mysterious and peaceful noise of the frogs and birds which reminded of him.
Of His sensual kiss
Only for her

She began to feel her stomach turning upside down, to sweating and feeling like throwing up. The belt's sign was lit and the passengers were asked to return to their seats. She run to the lavatory and began to vomit convulsively.
A powerful movement, then everything was over.

Saturday, at No Hour

Chapter ONE: The Big Bang?

"What is the transcendent? What is the soul?"

She had sat on the edge of the bed staring at the book. A piece of paper was sticking out between pages. She looked more carefully.

"That paper" and she continued "was it... could it really be possible?"

She opened the book where the paper was. Her heart started to beat faster.

. . . .

1:53, A few Days ago

About quantum teleportation

"If two electrons vibrate instantly in a state of coherence they can remain in a wave synchronization even if they are separated by light years.

There is however a "quantum interconnection" even the idea that particles vibrate coherent connected by a kind of deep connection." (Kaku, M., Physics of Impossible, 115)

Before leaving he had showed her a distant point on the map, a shore to the sea. Now they were in a garage in the basement of a big, grey building, totally opposed to what she expected to see. She insisted to go to the beach.

"It is too hot", he said.

He was right. She was no longer used to high temperatures of a common summer. She realized that she would not have coped with such heat, with the ocean waves. With the breeze of the sea, surrounded by hot sand covering her ankles... It would have been awful... pleasant.

A feeling of anxiety started to torment her as soon they arrived in front of the restaurant.

She had had her own reason to have such premonition, but deep inside she hoped things would be different. Last time they made plans about going down town but they chose the outdoor instead. She wanted to know him, to talk.

"Maybe this is how it was meant to be. You cannot decide when falling in love. It just happens" she thought.

They kept on walking without saying a word. And then the rest of the day, the rest of the journey, he proved her he knew things about her.

And she wondered

. . . .

What she read when she opened the book made her deeper engrossed in thought.

"The Star Gate was the codename for several secret telepathy studies, remote surveillance, sponsored by the CIA." "One of the most accurate, but also controversial studies, regarding the psycho kinetics, was performed within a program while searching whether the human mind, only by pure force of thought, was capable to affect the random results." (Kaku, M., Physics of Impossible, 134, 170)

!

She stopped. In the window a child size doll with a skull hanging on its hand, stared at her. The pink-yellow bras shredded into pieces, hung on the top of a rusty chandelier that was lying on the pedestal behind the doll. Next to the doll, on a boot punched by holes, there were two long bones sticking out.

"Agent? Him!? Are you kidding me? Why? For who? I assume it is a silly question but if he knew things... He seemed to know things about me, it's true. But thinking of everything that had happened so far"

She didn't have time to go on. The stifled noise had come from somewhere close. She turned around. At the last moment she had succeeded to catch sight of a shadow vanishing around the corner.

Unexpectedly the street light started to flicker. It was all she was able to see before everything became shrouded in total darkness.

"Strange. That doll in the corner of the window, it looked like a child. So real" she thought seemingly without any reason. A pain in the back of the head, and everything disappeared before she collapsed in a foul-smelling puddle.

....

"Things happen for a certain reason" he had said.

That day, in the car, when returning from the little town, was like no other before. They were speaking without saying a word, and yet they were communicating. She understood what he was thinking of, and it seemed that he could read her mind. They were thinking about the same things, uttering the same unspoken words. They were like one being. A unity. One singularity. That moment when they made love without touching each other, just thinking. That moment

"Do I think too loud?" he asked her.

"No, not really" she answered barely heard. She looked down and felt blushing.

He gave her the map, and then added:

"The guy who gave you the map seems to be nice, doesn't he?"

"Yes, I suppose so" she said quietly.

They continued to drive towards the sunset.

"So he must have known something about me. But how?"

When the door of the restaurant opened, she realized what was going to happen. His clothes should have revealed to her what he had planned; the light summer shirt in discrete colors, the elegant sun hat.

For a moment she could see inside the restaurant. The noise seemed to be hellish. She felt a hollow in her stomach followed by a striking pain. She suddenly turned and walked out, apologizing for not being properly dressed. It was true. She had dressed thinking that they would go to the sea-side, to chat. Or just to be quiet. She got a little mad at him because he had not told her what he had had in mind. Maybe she would have worn something else, not because she would have had a great choice, however.

"Don't worry, he said, it's just casual!"

Late night... @:

"Jacob paid 100 pieces of silver. Jacob built an altar there to worship God. Jacob named the place "EL (He)", the God..." (GENESIS, 33:5-34:12) (Holy Bible, Genesis, Easy- to- read version, 1989)

She remembered the day when they stopped in front of that Chinese restaurant and he had asked her money for the parking fare. Then at the pizzeria when it was her turn to pay. She had to be fair.

The cemetery was simple, with few ornaments and signs to remember the presence of the graves.

They had sat down on the grass without thinking if it was decent or not. She had waited to see how he would react. She knew him to be a Christian, and in a way, she was testing him. Maybe it was a way to get revenge. She had started talking fast, to tell him that she actually would have wanted to get to know him, to try to understand the meaning of things, and she had hoped that he would help her.

A woman with a child carrying a bouquet of flowers had shown up behind them, interrupting their conversation. They had laid the flowers on one of the graves and continued staring in silence.

She had asked him to go somewhere, to a smaller, more intimate, restaurant. And wished they had been alone. Had she been selfish? She had only thought of her own self perhaps, ignoring what he would have wanted. In fact she realized how it would have been in a place like that.

Only She and He

....

She had gone in and out several times in the airport's waiting lounge.

The first thought was to drink water. She could barely say two words. The temperature outside was way higher than she was used to. She headed to the information desk. The place was nearly deserted.

"If only I hadn't taken that map, if I hadn't talked, hadn't made a sound"

She looked around again. Most of the people that had come on same plane had disappeared in the airport's underground or in cabs. The moment she stepped outside the airport the wave of heat hit her ruthlessly. She felt her breath stop.

She had returned to the airport's lounge, sat down on one of the empty seats and waited.

"Do you need a cab, ma'am? I can take you wherever you want"

The 4ᵗʰ of…, never mind, 9:81!

"The string theory was a "seat-of-your-pants" method, guessing the answers. Such short cuts were not supposed to be possible" (Kaku, M., Parallel Worlds, 189)

The day was hot and still she had gone out. The area was a field split by a railway. A rusty train had been waiting for a long time for the departure signal.

"Forbidden area!" she read. "Is the zone truly forbidden? It does look abandoned to me"

She imagined how, by stepping across the rails between wagons, she would have got there, to the store. But she gave up. What she could see through the line of wagons were piles of dirt and debris in endless rows. She turned down the same way she had come. A large, vivid black spotted,butterfly had suddenly appeared. Then birds. Then insects. And more butterflies.

The spot was higher than the surroundings and nothing seemed to grow on it. It reminded her of an underground deposit where non environmentally friendly materials were supposed to have been stored.

"Not a very healthy place" she said and tried to bypass it by following the vegetation.

Her feet sunk in the soft clay and she almost got stuck. She realized she had no choice. Without too much enthusiasm she turned around and started to cross the deserted area. There were not only monster butterflies now but also enormous flies and bugs surrounding her as if they were dancing in the insufferable heat. She was thirsty and wished so much she could drink. Water.

A lot of water.

Zebras

He had told her how he used to walk along the river that separated the two counties, that he liked taking photos. Then they had got to the bridge. It was the same one. Blue. He had shown her the day before, in one of the photos.

It had started to rain. They had gone along the main street unhindered by the splashing raindrops. There, in a small shop she had bought the scarf. She liked it so much that she couldn't resist the impulse to buy it.

The boutique was coquettish. Things were scattered in two small rooms separated by three steps. She was fascinated. They walked around for a while trying to find something that she might like. She let her gaze wander over space and time. The transparent scarf was delicate like a spider web. She had already decided to buy it but she still went on asking him:

"Well what do you think about it?"

"You know, I'm not too interested in such things" he said.

"You should not necessarily be interested" she replied while putting the scarf over her shoulders, admiring herself in the large wall mirror.

He was already seated in one of the chairs that served as décor, proudly admiring his acquisition: an iron crock. She sat next to him. On the back of the chair there were two pieces of fabric. White, with black stripes. Or maybe black, with white stripes.

"What does actually a zebra look like? White with black stripes, or black with white stripes?" she asked.

"I really don't know" he replied. After a moment he said:

"I love it. It's really you." and continued watching her.

Thursday, the 14th, at 3 pm

To my friend

"Spirits want to meet you. You must be undefended so that you can accept such an invitation. When you seek something, begin with your heart. The cave of the heart is the home of truth." (Adapted after Deepak Chopra)

"So you really think that God is just an idea?" he asked her.
"Yes, I do" and looked at him as if she had defeated him in a battle of ideas.

She had succeeded in making him doubt about what he had strongly believed in by then. She really enjoyed these types of discussion, in contradiction, and she really liked being number one.

"I shall think about that" he said looking intensely ahead.

It was late midnight and they hadn't met any car by then. The moment they had hit the road she saw a flash. A car accident. She hurried to fasten the belt and he did the same without commenting about it. She was thinking she had to talk to him, to say something interesting so that he could be alert. The only topic that occurred in her mind was about God. She was an amateur when discussing about religion but this thing didn't prevent her from stating her point of view.

"I really don't understand why do I have to go to someone else to tell me what to think, what to believe in. What and how to do, to be a good person. I have a brain. I can think for myself. Don't you think so?" she said and spied on him discretely to see his reaction.

A fugitive smile passed on his tired face.

They stopped at an internet café. Even though she did not ordered anything she couldn't stop herself from having a sip from his hot coffee and a bite from the honey cake. He watched her without saying a word but his eyes seemed to agree in a mutual complicity. In the last moment they gave up the research on the internet and they were headed towards the beach.

"It didn't take so much time to drive back. Why?" she asked him.

"Well, you know..." he said, "it's like that, you know..." and he didn't continue.

"Well I don't. Tell me!" she said.

He didn't know what to answer. She leaned over and kissed him. Once. Twice

Then they talked about God, about talking about God

About

00:01

To: ME

Magical and miraculous

"Coincidences are messages from your soul; they are clues to the nonlocal Self. When coincidence happens, in that moment you have glimpsed your soul." (Adapted after Deepak Chopra, Power, Freedom, and Grace, Amber-Allen Publishing Inc., 2006)

Tachyons

If they had existed or if they still exist, in the process of sending and receiving information, then space, and I mean the matter in the universe, would be nothing but a sea of information. From the beginning of the beginning, up to now, in the present. Or future.

If there were tachyons, this would mean that the existent information around us, or the supposed existent one, represents both past and future.

If what we see now, that galaxies are getting further away from each other, would be in fact something that had already happened, this would mean that what we see is happening in what we call "our reality", is the opposite phenomenon, that of galaxies coming nearer to each other. And space is collapsing.

If tachyons exist, or ever existed, since the beginning of the beginnings, it doesn't mean that…In the moment a tachyon is emitted one with opposite charge is absorbed then

The Universe. If the Universe would be a sea of information that bends, and this information would be distorted scattered by the "folding" of space, a metaphysical folding determined by obstacles in the space-time system (remains of, or after, the primordial opening), then…

If space were stretched and linear like a piece of paper, it would be easier to receive information. This would mean that tachyons don't have a linear path but follow the curve of T-Space. This would mean that information sent with the help of tachyons would be distorted because of the space irregularities. Mathematically speaking, the factor, or the coefficient thatshould be added to the mathematics calculations in this case would be... I have no idea. Wait!

IF the Universe were a sea of information maybe this information would look like ONE and ZEROS, or strings of DNA.

And IF the information in the Universe were strings of DNA, or strings of tachyons which travel in time, it could explain the biodiversity on our planet. Think about the way organisms have adapted to the existing environment, transforming it! This means that we are definitely not alone in the universe.

IF everything around us is Matter in various forms, at various Energy levels, this would mean that matter organizes according to the received information by finding the most probable balance/energy levelof the system.

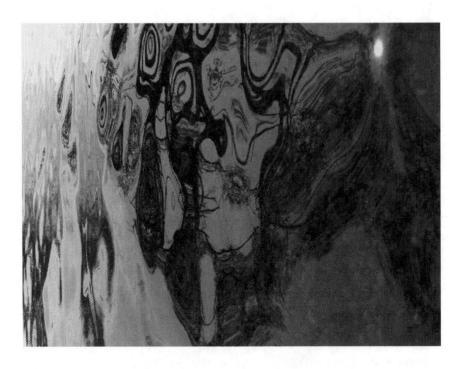

Imagine fields of strings of informational DNA,
Time and Space Travelling Matter.

The information reaches a planet someday. The matter containing these informational strings has ordered itself so well that after millions of years of evolution, has managed to be compatible with its own "perpetuum mobile" environmental conditions.

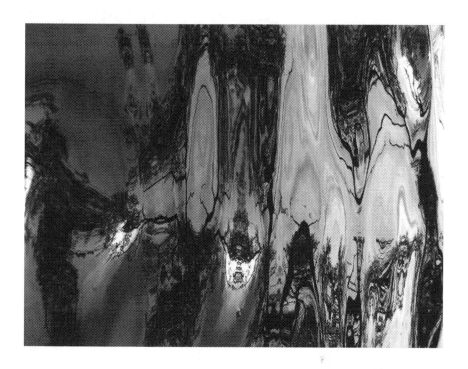

And if information were both strings of DNA
and Ones and Zeroes then...

In analogy with the visual presentations which define the world of computers by representing the information transmitted between 2 marks by codes then we can easily assume that what we have around us, in macro and micro universes, are fields of coded matter.

If matter organizes itself, and finds by itself the most balanced energetic forms, this would mean that matter has its own consciousness.

That it is conscious! How cool is that, right?

Please, no need to hurry up like that. You will
all get my autograph. There is plenty of

TIME

2: me

Hello,

About me:

If I were to tell you just one thing about me, I'd tell you that I'm a Christian. This is the most significant thing about me. I believe in God, and in Jesus Christ, and the Holy Spirit – the three manifestations of God. We can discuss more about it, or, if you wish, we can talk about it later. But my faith in God is a standard for my whole thinking and behavior.

Of course that doesn't mean I always lived at the height of this standard. Most nonbelievers think that if you fail in your attempt to live at the height of this standard, you become a hypocrite. And this is what most people use as a reason to reject the whole idea about God. But the truth is that living for God and believing in His truth, represents a fight fought over the course of an entire life and no one realizes that we are simply incapable to complete this objective, to reach this level of perfection. It's not hypocrisy. But more about that later on.

About you and me:

I feel guilty about what happened Saturday night. I did not plan something like that to happen. But I've been alone and without women for a long time. I felt you wanted me so I let it happen. I liked it. But I think it was something crazy, because you are a woman I don't know. Despite all this, I've left myself attracted to you, when I really didn't want that thing to happen. Now I'm trying to decide what to do. You say that sometimes people just think too much and let things get out of their control. Maybe. But what happened was a very intimate thing (the most intimate) and I'm not so used to this way.

Your friend

"Raise your right hand ma'am" the policeman said.

"Do you swear to tell the truth, the whole truth and nothing but the truth?"

She turned her head and looked at the row to her right. The girl's face with big, deep blue eyes, light chestnut hair reaching to her small, frail shoulders, the smile she got the moment she looked at her, the front teeth missing. She then looked at the judge, with her right hand raised, standing firm and decided. In that moment she thought about her own child whom she hadn't seen for so long:

"I do!"

00:00

"Who was he? How was he?" she wondered, and looked outside for a second, and then a third time.

"Maybe I could speak to him, and we could discuss. Maybe we would try knowing each other"

"I and He"

She was all ready when the phone rang. At least that's what she thought. She went back twice to make sure that everything was alright.

Then she met him. For the first time

And HE called HER

MAYA

On the Bridge. At eight pm

Maybe it won't rain. I can still do a few laps. I really need to move my legs. One day I will start to run. I know I will miss the marathon this time, but maybe next year.

This team of trainers seems like they are new. And quite young. Big too. Wonder if they train football. Let's see who is coming now. Two ladies and a girl. Never seen before. And my friend? He's not here. Strange, he used to be on the track at this time. It is surprising how he can still keep moving. So much energy. At his age! It's impressive I must admit. He must be seventy or so. He always walks the opposite direction than the others.

In fact it is the best way to meet people, to see their faces and make contact otherwise the only thing you see is the back side, the butts, which is funny because you always can compare them and make a "top ten" award list. And then the way they move and shake their buttocks! I thought it was only women that are funny when walking, but guys can also be funny. Really funny. It was that guy, a quite young man, relatively big, tall, and fleshy that was running. It looked like he was swimming. His head was leaning ahead quite a bit but enough for not falling and smashing it into a flat oversize pumpkin, while his arms had their own destiny. From behind it looked like he had two shuffles making his way through the air. Or it looked more like a rooster, waving his wings when looking for... I don't know what. A chick, maybe?!

- Ok. Rain, please! Now! It's the time. Soon she'll be here. Are you ready? Come on! Don't waste more time or they will miss each other.

Damn it! It started to rain. I only managed to do two laps. Maybe tomorrow will be better weather. Well, I need to get some parsley and sugar anyway. And it's getting late. Curious there is no traffic on the highway. Usually there are a lot of cars this time of the day.

"Excuse me! Excuse me!"

"Yes?!"

"Can you tell me please where the bus stop is?"

"You have to go back. You were going in the wrong direction. If you go back a few, then at the next cross road you should …. You know what, I can take you there. I live around here."

"How long have you been here? Is it far your place?"

"One year. No, not really."

"One year? Doing what?"

"Writing. A book. And you?"

"I am playing the violin."

"Really!? So you were coming from a concert. Your accent is… Where do you come from?"

"Yours too. I am from A. And you?"

"B. It's almost the same country. Neighbors! Funny. How strange life is some times. We both have traveled thousands of miles. To meet here. On the bridge. At eight pm."

- More rain?

- No. It's not necessary. We needed it just to get her out of the track otherwise they would have missed each other.

- Sure?

- Yeah. No need for more rain for now. Let see what will happen next.

- Ok!

References

Chopra, D. (1998). *Ageless Body, Timeless Mind.* Thee Rivers Press.

Chopra, D. (2000). *How To Know God.* Harmony Books.

Chopra, D. (2004). *The Book of Secrets.* London: Rider.

Chopra, D. (2006). *Power, Freedom and Grace.* Amber-Allen Publishing Inc.

Chopra, D. (2006). *The Kama Sutra.* Virgin Books.

Chopra, D. (2009). *Reinventing the Body, Resurecting the Soul.* Harmony Books.

Damasio, A. (1999). *Review of The Feelingof What Happens: Body, Emotion and the Making of consciousness.* Harcourt.

Holy Bible, Genesis, Easy- to- read version. (1989). World Bible.

Kaku, M. (2004). *Parallel Worlds.* USA: Doubleday.

Kaku, M. (2008). *Physics of the Impossible.* USA: Doubleday Publishing.

Sears, F. Z. (u.d.). *Fizica.* Wesley Publishing Comp., Editura Didactica si Pedagogica.